DRAGON TALES

TERESA LEIGH JUDD

Dragon Tales

Formatted by IRONHORSE formatting

ISBN: 1499126328
ISBN-13: 978-1499126327

DEDICATION

This book is dedicated to my three great kids, Gretchen, Tom and Trish, who are always there for me when I need them. I'm proud of you all.

SPECIAL ACKNOWLEDGEMENTS

Thanks to my critique group, Cindy, Kathy, Pat and Rae, without whose help and advice this "dream" would never have come true.

And to:

Karen Phillips for the cover design –
www.PhillipsCovers.com

Ken Dahms for dragon art

CONTENTS

A DREAM COME TRUE

Marcia sat at her kitchen table sipping her first cup of coffee for the day. *She was so tired!* She couldn't remember the last time she had gotten a good night's sleep. It took a large amount of caffeine plus a brisk shower to get her started every morning. Not that she was all that excited about plunging into a day of retail sales in any case. *This is what she got a degree in marketing for?*

Worst of all, her sleep was being interrupted by the same dream every night. A huge fire-breathing dragon hovered over her. The heat from the dragon's mouth scorched her skin, his red eyes drilled into her, and his green scaly body blocked all escape. She would sit upright in fear, face sweaty, heart palpitating, and then realize it was just a dream. Gradually she'd sink back into slumber, but it was fitful and erratic, and when she awoke the next morning, she was deathly tired. *Why wouldn't this dream go away? It wasn't like dragons were real, and even if they did exist somewhere, she didn't know any personally. Very funny, Marcia. Obviously, the lack of sleep was getting to her.*

Getting up from the table, she retrieved the book on dream interpretation she had purchased the day before. She'd felt ridiculous buying it, but she'd thought just maybe it could help her find out why she was having these "dragon" dreams. Anything to make them go away.

She leafed through the book until she found the chapter she needed. "Dreaming of Dragons," the caption read. *Well, that would certainly be her*.

"You will get an enormous boost in your progress toward financial success from a powerful and influential personage, and if you don't now know such a VIP, you will soon."

Well, that would be great, just not likely. No rich influential people in her immediate circle. And, she just wasted $6.95 on the stupid book.

Slapping it down on the table, she dragged herself to the bathroom, showered and dressed in the obligatory "business" attire of a cosmetic company representative. She paid special attention to her makeup, wishing it wasn't so important. A glance in the mirror revealed the perfect eyeliner, the perfect mascara, the perfect lipstick. With a deep sigh, she grabbed her car keys and made tracks for the mall where she would stand behind a counter for the better part of the day. She couldn't afford to be late. She couldn't afford to lose her pathetic job.

As the day dragged by, she smiled and smiled and smiled, encouraging hesitant customers into sitting for a "makeover." Telling them how this or that product would enhance their eyes or their skin color. Not telling them she bought her own cosmetics at the local drug store. Even with the discount, she couldn't afford the prices at the department store. Dreaming of a high paying job in business, she had invested everything into a degree at the local college. But when she graduated, there had been no jobs available. The recession made even finding a retail clerk job difficult, and she still had student loans to repay.

Some of her friends were getting help from their parents, but Marcia's parents were dead. She had no living relatives. She had made her way through school by waitressing at a local sports bar. At twenty-four, it seemed her prospects were shrinking instead of expanding. A long life of drudgery stretched before her. This was definitely not the future she had planned when she had completed her studies and set off with high hopes and a diploma in hand.

Eight hours on her feet in high heels were almost all she could bear. *Why high heels any way? Who made these rules? Obviously a man.* Now, after seemingly endless hours behind a glass counter in Walker's Emporium, she sighed as she sank into a booth across from her best friend, Betts, at their local watering hole. Kicking off her shoes under the table, she held up her hand as the waiter approached and ordered a glass of red wine. Betts already had a glass of wine in front of her and was obviously anxious to catch up on the latest gossip. Since it had been another day without anything of note happening in her life, Marcia asked first.

"Any luck finding a job?"

"Nope," Betts answered. "Meet any millionaires behind the cosmetic counter?"

"Why do you ask? Have you been reading my dream interpretation book?"

"You have a dream interpretation book?"

Marcia looked sheepish. "I did buy one. I keep having this stupid dream about a dragon, a big green guy with red eyes. You know, I told you the dream has been waking me up every night. I thought maybe I could find out why I was having them."

"And?"

"It was just some mumbo-jumbo about meeting someone who would bring me financial success. Yeah, right. Kind of on a par with the daily horoscopes in the newspaper. Oh, thanks," she said to the waiter, who had arrived with her drink.

"Well, I have an idea," Betts said. "We're both smart, attractive and educated. What we need to do is start a business of our own." Betts leaned back, exuding as much self satisfaction as if she had solved world hunger and eradicated war.

"What business did you have in mind? Door-to-door vacuum sales? Home parties selling jewelry? I mean what? We can't cook. Aren't trained to decorate homes. I can't even sew. I mean, what?"

"Personal organizers."

"Personal organizers, what are those?"

"You know. People who go into other peoples' homes and sort and organize their stuff."

"It has been my experience that people who have a lot of junk, don't really want to get rid of it and only do so when they're on TV."

"Be that as it may, I have our first job already lined up."

"You so have to be kidding."

"Nope. One of my friends told me about this guy, John Lambert, who inherited a house from his aunt. He says he doesn't have time to deal with it, there's so much stuff. Wants us to clear it out and organize it. I told him I'd give him a good rate since we could only work on weekends. He said he was in no hurry."

"Whoa, Whoa. Do we know what we're getting into?"

"He gave me a key so I went ahead and looked at the house," Betts said. "It's not too bad. She wasn't a hoarder or anything, just an old lady with a lot of stuff. I mean, how hard can it be? A pile for trash, a pile for the

Goodwill and a pile for him to go through and decide what he would like to keep. We start on Saturday. It could be fun seeing what someone else has accumulated."

"You might be right. Okay, I'm in." Marcia sipped her wine. "This guy isn't hot by any chance, is he?"

"No such luck. Middle-aged, a little dumpy looking."

"Oh, well, it was just a thought," Marcia sighed.

Saturday morning, dressed in an old shirt and jeans, Marcia met Betts in front of a one-story wood house in a middle-class neighborhood. Paint could be seen peeling off the exterior in some places and the yard consisted mostly of weeds. The houses on either side were struggling to keep up appearances and property values, but the occupant of this house had obviously given up the fight.

Betts unlocked the front door and Marcia followed her in. It wasn't too bad, a lot of old furniture and knick knacks, but no narrow trails through walls of newspaper.

"Let's start in the kitchen." Betts led the way. "John said he came in and threw out all the perishables so it wouldn't get to smelling bad in here."

A couple hours later, they had two paper grocery bags of unopened food as well as several large plastic bags of disposable items neatly lined up in the foyer.

Betts picked up one of the bags. "I'll take the useable items to the food bank. Back in a jif."

"Okay. I'll start cleaning and organizing the dishes." Marcia opened the nearest cupboard and surveyed the contents. By the time Betts got back, the kitchen was looking neat and clean though the avocado green appliances all screamed the sixties. "I think we're done for the day," Marcia said. "I'm going to take some of the towels and linens, including the curtains, home and wash them. Tomorrow we can start on one of the other rooms."

"Good plan. Want to come by for a drink on the way home?"

"No, thanks. I'm bushed, but I have to say this is a rewarding job. Just look at what we've accomplished in one day!" She spread out her arms and twirled around. *Maybe, just maybe, this could work.*

The next morning, they were both at the house, eager to begin.

"Hey, this is kind of fun," Marcia said.

"Told you so."

"Okay, you take one back bedroom and I'll take the other."

Betts took the bedroom the woman obviously used. Dark bedstead, side tables, a bureau and lots of clothes in the closet. Marcia took one look at the other room and realized that it was more a storage space than a bedroom. They both grabbed big plastic bags and set to work.

Marcia waded through boxes of fabric, skeins of yarn and an alarming amount of dust. As she came around a tall stack of boxes, she jumped back in alarm. A gray figure was huddled in a corner. Closer inspection revealed it to be an old dress form topped with a hat. She laughed at herself, but it took awhile before her heart slowed down to normal.

A couple hours later, Betts called from the other room. "Hey, I'm going to McDonalds to pick up lunch. What do you want?"

"I'll take a crispy chicken sandwich and a diet coke. Thanks."

"Fries?"

"No, I'd better not. Can't afford to buy a larger size wardrobe," Marcia laughed.

Betts grabbed a couple of trash bags and left, heaving them into the dumpster looming in the driveway on the way to her car. The owner had agreed to pay for it, and it was certainly more practical than lugging numerous bags to the dump.

While Betts was gone, Marcia worked her way deeper into the spare room until she reached an old bureau set against the wall. She started pulling out drawers. They were stuffed full with a hodgepodge of unused items that might be needed some day: packs of emery boards, expired cosmetics, shampoo and conditioner samples, extra scissors and tweezers. The bottom drawer was larger and much heavier than those above it. Marcia heaved it open and stared down into a fairly empty space with just a few kitchen towels piled inside. Given the weight of the drawer, it didn't make any sense. Looking more closely, she saw that the drawer was extremely shallow on the inside and quite deep on the outside.

She pulled the drawer completely out of the bureau and set it on the floor. Removing the towels, she stared into what looked like an empty drawer, but she could see that it was just a false bottom. Using a pair of scissors, she pried up the board and gazed at the contents in shock. There were stacks of money. Hundreds of dollars banded together. Apparently the old woman hadn't believed in banks.

Marcia sat back on her haunches and thought about all the possible uses for so much money. She could pay off her loans, invest in their new venture, quit her job. *Was honesty the best policy? Who would ever know if she took it?*

Hearing the front door open, she quickly pushed the drawer back in place.

"Hi, Honey, I'm home," Betts called.

Then a man's voice could be heard laughing.

"And I brought company."

Marcia, her face a little red from her exertions, walked into the living room and found a tall, attractive man standing behind Betts. She started quickly trying to push her straggly hair into some semblance of order, at the same time brushing dust from her jeans. She hadn't even bothered to put on makeup that morning and had on her oldest clothes. Not a great first impression.

"Hi," she said.

"Hi, yourself. You must be Marcia, the other part of the dynamic duo. I'm John Lambert. Thought I'd stop by and see how things were going. It looks like you're making great progress."

"It's so nice to meet you. Actually, we're really enjoying the job."

"I'm glad to hear it. I like the idea of helping a small enterprise get off the ground."

"Are you planning on living here when we're finished?" Marcia asked.

"Live here? Hardly. I'll either sell or rent. Not my kind of space, if you know what I mean. Well, I'm outta here. I'll check back later. Keep up the good work."

"Bye, nice meeting you," Marcia said and then turned on her friend. "What were you thinking? He's great looking and nice. Were you keeping him for yourself?"

"No, no, nothing like that. He's just a friend of a friend."

"So-o-o, you were just keeping him a secret? For what reason?"

"I knew you'd meet him and be all over him. I wanted to get the job started first."

"All over him? What am I, an octopus?"

"You're right. It was a mean trick. It was funny, seeing your face though."

"What does he do for a living?"

"Some kind of investment banker, I think."

"Like in my dragon dreams book?"

"If you'd like to think so."

After that, they munched their sandwiches, sipped their cokes and tossed the take-out bags into the dumpster.

"I'm going back to work on my room now," Marcia announced. She was in a quandary about what to do with all the money she had found, but until she knew what to do with it she wanted to make sure it was well hidden.

At the end of the day, she still hadn't decided what to do. The two of them locked up and went home for some much needed rest. Monday morning loomed ahead of them.

Marcia couldn't keep away from what she now thought of as *her* money. With the extra key Betts had made for her, she took to checking on it in the evenings. It was always there, safe in its little hiding place. It occurred to her that the dragon dream might have been right. She may have met the person who was to bring her financial success. He just didn't know that he had. Who would she be hurting if she kept it? It was found money. No one knew about it. John Lambert seemed wealthy in his own right and probably didn't need it. While she and Betts could really use it to boost their new business. By Thursday night, she had made her decision. Counting the bills, she shoved them into the large duffle bag she had brought from home. It was over one hundred thousand dollars. She was rich.

The next day she called Betts. "Meet me for drinks tonight?"

"Sounds good. See you then."

With a big smile, Marcia slid into the booth across from her friend and ordered her usual glass of wine from the waiter.

"What's up?" Betts asked. "You sounded really up when you called. Did your dragons finally bring you a pot of gold?"

"That's leprechauns, doofus. But here's the thing. I've decided to quit my job and go into the personal organizer business full-time. I'm giving two weeks notice on Monday. I want to get some books on organization, maybe have John help us set up a business plan and start advertising."

"Marcia. I know this job is working out well, but what if we don't get enough jobs at first. What will you live on if you quit?"

"I didn't say anything before, but I recently received a small inheritance from an aunt." *It wasn't a lie, it just wasn't her aunt.*

"Really? That's wonderful. Let's go for it."

A few months later, the two women were busy working on their latest project. Business was growing and they were now showing a profit.

During a break, Betts asked, "Marcia, are you feeling all right? You don't look very good."

"Gee, thanks a lot."

"No, really, are you ill?"

"I'm fine. You're just not used to seeing me without the cosmetics I used to wear for work. And, I have to admit I'm still not sleeping very well. Those darn dragons. There used to be just one. Now there are more every night."

"If you're sure … Still, maybe you should make a doctor's appointment. Your eyes look red and there's sort of a greenish tint to your skin."

THE PRINCESS WHO LOVED DRAGONS

"What is it with you and dragons, Princess?" Michelle's father asked, taking a jadeite carving down from the mantelpiece and turning it over in his hand. After admiring it for a minute, he carefully placed it back in position.

Michelle gazed around the room, her eye lighting on one of the more ornate figurines, enjoying the way the firelight glinted off its gold border.

"I don't know, Dad, I just like them so I collect them. And don't call me 'Princess'. I'm not ten years old anymore. I'm in my thirties. Call me by my real name."

"Sorry. Old habits die hard. It just seems like there are more dragons every time I come to dinner."

"Well, you're right. I have been getting a few more. Once I really looked at one, I began to notice them everywhere. They are so intricate, so beautiful, and besides they're supposed to bring good luck."

"But dragons are fearsome creatures who breathe fire."

"Not all of them. What about Puff?"

"Puff aside, the rest of them have a rather unsavory reputation. All that capturing of fair maiden stuff. Knights in armor dashing to the rescue. It's in a lot of books so it must be true."

Michelle laughed. "I'm beyond the fair maiden stage, Dad. And I don't think dragons are much of a threat to old maids."

"You aren't an old maid. Look at you. You're pretty, smart, accomplished. You just haven't found the right dragon slayer yet."

"Enough about dragons already. Dinner is served." Michelle set plates of steaming pasta at each of their places and poured rich red wine into two goblets. The once-a-month ritual of dinner with her father, which had started shortly after her mother died, was an event to be looked forward to, their own special father and daughter connection.

"So what else have you been up to besides acquiring dragons?" her father asked.

"Same old, same old," she answered. Although her job as a librarian gave her access to the universe and all it encompassed, for all intents and purposes she was locked into a small brick building in an even smaller town. Her real life travels took her only as far as the front door of her house and back.

"You need to get out more," her father said, bringing her back to the present.

"I know. It just seems like there's no time. And fixing up this house is taking all my money right now. Maybe I can take a trip next summer."

After dinner, they carried their wine glasses into the living room of her newly-purchased house and sat with their feet up on the coffee table in front of the fireplace. They laughed and reminisced about a time when she was a child and he was a young man. It made them both feel good to revisit memories of the past.

"Well, Princess, I had better be going," her father said, standing and setting his glass down on the table. "As usual it was a wonderful evening."

"Da-a-d!"

"Oh, sorry ~ it was a wonderful evening, *Michelle*. But in spite of your being all grown up, you're still a princess to me."

"What can I say to that? You know I always enjoy our visits so if you want to call me Princess, so be it. Goodnight now, drive safely," Michelle said as she kissed him on his cheek.

"Goodnight. Oh, and have someone look at your heater. I think it's malfunctioning. It's awfully cold in your house."

"The heater's fine. The house is just drafty, but the fireplace makes up for it."

She stood in the doorway and waved goodbye as he got into his car and backed out of the driveway, smiling to herself. He never stopped parenting in spite of the fact that she was well beyond needing it. Yes, her house was in need of work, but it was what she could afford and she was proud of being a homeowner. Slowly, she had begun to repair and remodel. She didn't need to travel, each project was an adventure, and she was enjoying every one of them.

Back in the house, she turned out the lights. The fire in the fireplace was barely smoldering and a chill had already begun to invade the room. She quickly washed her face, brushed her teeth and, donning a flannel nightgown, jumped into bed. Pulling the comforter over her, she laughed to herself about her father's dragon remarks and fell soundly asleep.

She knew she was dreaming, but she couldn't seem to wake up. She was dressed in a flowing white gown, standing with her back against a tree, unable to move. A huge dragon stood in front of her belching fire from his nostrils. The heat from his breath was almost unendurable. Shaking with fear, she twisted and turned, trying to escape. Hot, she was too hot. She had to get away. Struggling, she awoke and found she was wound tightly in the bedding. Most nights the house was so cold she huddled under the covers just to keep warm enough to sleep. She threw off the blankets and immediately realized that the room itself was hot.

She sat up and looked around. Smoke was pouring in from the living room. A low roaring noise filled her ears. Fire! She jumped out of bed and ran to the door. Flames reached out to engulf her when she opened it. She slammed the door shut and ran to the window. Never having been opened, she found it was painted shut. She groped for the metal dragon on her bedside table, grabbed it and smashed the window. Fresh air poured in. But the space was too small for her to crawl through. Glass shards cut her arms as she tried to break open a bigger hole. Blood ran down her arms as fingers of smoke crept around the doorframe. She began to lose consciousness.

When she came to, she was being carried from the blazing building in the arms of a firefighter. She looked up into his handsome face, and as the flames' reflection danced across his helmet, she realized that she had indeed been rescued by a knight in shining armor.

Previously published March 2010 online in Long and Short Review.

A SAFE PLACE

Julie watched as her eight-year-old daughter, Emma, blue eyes bright with excitement and unruly blonde curls bobbing, raced across the open field. Her arms held high, she played out string as her kite slowly rose off the ground. Catching a breeze, it began to soar upward. It was their newest acquisition, a beautiful Chinese dragon decorating its crimson face, a long red and yellow tail trailing behind. The kite rose higher and higher, dipping and swaying in the air currents and moving ever closer to the woods bordering the field.

Suddenly, as if drawn by an invisible force, it began to drop, falling like a dead weight until it vanished into the trees.

Emma stood forlorn in the midst of the field, her hands clutching the now slack string.

"Come on, Emma." Julie started towards the woods. "We can find it."

"No, Mom! We can't go in there!"

"Why not?"

"Don't you know?" Emma said, lowering her voice almost to a whisper. "That's where little children go to disappear."

"Don't be silly. That's not possible."

"Mom, everyone at school says that kids disappear if they go in there."

"Everyone says?"

"Yes. Let's forget the kite and go home." Emma dropped the string, turned her back to the field and marched determinedly away.

"Well, okay, if you feel that strongly about it." Julie gathered their things and followed her.

Once they were home, Julie brought up the subject again.

"What have you heard about those woods, Emma?"

"Just what they say at school. A couple of kids went missing there awhile back."

Julie let the subject drop but mentally made a note to check into it.

Julie and her daughter, Emma, had only recently moved to Lost Pines in the foothills of California. Widowed at the age of thirty four, at first Julie was at a loss as to how to provide enough income to support the two of them. But falling back on a college degree in Library Science, she felt extremely lucky to have landed a job as librarian in the small rural town and doubly lucky to have found a cottage that she could afford to buy. The work was routine and not at all demanding. She had met a number of the local residents and was welcomed warmly by all. And even more important, Emma had blossomed in the laid back environment so different from the harsh and often cruel big city school system from which they had come.

Monday morning as she unlocked the front doors to the little library, Julie smiled to herself. She had gotten the perfect job in the perfect town. Things were definitely looking up.

Throughout the morning, the occasional customer came and went, checking out the week's reading materials, but no one that she knew at all well. Finally, she spied the owner of the local market, a round cheerful woman with gray hair sprayed into what looked like a medieval helmet, bustling in the door.

"Hi, Mrs. Owens, how are you today?" Julie asked.

"Oh, just fine. Thought I'd look through the mysteries. Get any new ones?"

"Yes. I just shelved quite a few. Were you looking for any author in particular?"

"Oh, I have my favorites, all right. I'll just check for myself."

"Um, Mrs. Owens?"

"Yes?"

"I was wondering. Emma came home with some weird story about children going missing in the woods behind the Whitakers' farm. Did you ever hear anything like that?"

The woman visibly paled and took a step backward.

"No, no. Nothing like that happened here. This is a quiet village. Stuff like that only happens in big cities. You know how kids are. They listen to all those old ghost stories and then try to scare other kids." She looked at her watch and turned to go. "Oh, I'm late for work. They'll be wondering where I am."

"Didn't you want to get a book?"

"Oh, right. I'll have to come back later," she said, exiting the room as fast as possible, while glancing behind her as if she expected to be chased by demons.

Very strange, Julie thought. Given the way the woman had overreacted to her question, she decided to look through some of the old newspapers stored in the basement.

The basement turned out to be a nightmare of storage bins. The previous librarian, who had apparently left hurriedly for parts unknown, hadn't been good about keeping things in order. But, after batting down spider webs and raising a cloud of dust, Julie found the files and carried one of the boxes up to her desk. Copies of the newspaper had only been preserved on microfiche since the early 1950's and, with the talk about missing children, Julie thought that if anything had happened, it had probably been earlier than that. Still, the heavy books containing the actual older newspapers were daunting. She decided to try the microfiche first. It was going to be a big project, viewing so many years of old issues, especially since she had no idea what to look for or when to look. Still, she had time on her hands and was curious enough to try.

Luckily, it was a weekly paper, otherwise she didn't think she would have the strength to continue. She took an occasional break when someone came to the desk to check out a book and then went back to work, carefully filing the film in order as she finished each one. Rubbing her hands over her tired eyes as she scrolled through issue after issue, she despaired of finding anything. So far, although she had waded through most of the 1950s, she had spied nothing of note.

"Mommy." A little voice by her elbow startled her into attention. "What are you doing?"

"Emma, oh, my gosh, is school out already?"

"Yes. I came straight here like you told me to."

"What a good girl you are. Let me find you a book to read. I only have another hour before we close."

"What is that machine?"

"Oh, it's called a microfiche. It lets you read pages of old newspapers. I was making sure they were in order," Julie lied.

"Neat. Let me see."

Julie showed her how it worked and, curiosity satisfied, Emma took the book her mother handed her and settled into a nearby chair.

An hour later, Julie had finished the '50s. She glanced at the clock and realized it was after five. The building was empty, and her daughter, Emma, was engrossed in a book.

"Time to go home to dinner, Emma." Julie picked up her purse and started turning off the lights.

"Ok, Mom, I just have a little more to read."

"You can take the book home, honey. I'll bring it back in the morning."

"Is that cheating?"

"No. Since I'm the librarian, I can take books out when I want to," she said, smiling at her little play-by-the-rules child. "Let's go."

After dinner, Julie brought up the missing children question again.

"So, Emma, what did you hear about the children who disappeared?"

"Nothing. Everyone just says don't go in the woods. A monster lives there and eats little kids."

"I see. Did they say what little kids?"

"No. Just that they were a boy and girl, brother and sister. Went in there to explore and never came back."

"Did they say when this was?"

"No. A long time ago is all."

"A long time ago" for a little child could be as little as a year or distant history, Julie thought. Instead of searching old newspapers, she decided to pay a visit to the sheriff's office. Certainly someone there would know.

The next morning on her way to work, Julie stopped by the building that housed the sheriff's department. Inside she hesitated while she looked around for some sign of activity. A tall, lanky man in a beige uniform appeared from a door leading back to another room.

"Can I help you, Ma'am?"

"Um. I'm not sure. Are you the Sheriff?"

"Yep, that's me, Rick Johnson. And you are?"

"I'm the new librarian, Julie Lindstrom."

"What can I do for you, Julie?"

"Well, I know this sounds silly, but my little girl came home from school with a story about some children going missing near here. I just wanted to check it out."

"I haven't heard of anything like that, but I've only been here a couple months. After too many years of crime in the big city, I decided to move to a smaller, quieter community."

"What about the other officers here? Would they know?"

"Well, there's just one deputy, and he's only been here a month more than me. Same with the dispatcher – newly hired. I'll ask them though and let you know if I find out anything. I can find you at the library?"

"Yes. What about the City Council members? Maybe they know."

"Right. You could ask them."

"Can you tell me who they are?"

"There's Mr. Owens from the market, Jack Berger over to the barber shop, Olivia Redmond from the real estate office and old man Whitaker who owns a farm out past the woods, though I hear he's seldom seen in town. I think his wife comes in once a week to buy supplies. And, of course, the mayor, Bob Carter. His office is in that little building that serves as a makeshift city hall, where the DMV and the offices for building permits are."

"Thank you so much for all your help, Sheriff."

"I don't think I was much help, but missing children sounds serious so I'll certainly look into it. I'll come by the library if I find out anything."

"Thanks again," Julie said, looking at the clock on the wall. "I'd better get going or I'll be late opening up. Can't have a long line of patrons waiting outside the door, can I?"

Laughing, she stepped out onto the street and headed up the hill to the library building. On the way, she passed the real estate office and peered in, but it didn't look open. Probably not a lot of business in this town, but then again, she had already found three other people who had only just moved here. More turnover than one would expect.

Reviewing the city council members, she eliminated the store owner, Mr. Owens. He probably wouldn't be any more help than his wife. And the Whitakers lived too far out. That left the barber, the mayor and the real estate agent. She decided to try the mayor on her lunch break.

As the day went on, Julie continued to wade through the microfiche with no more success than the day before. Having finished the '50s, she was well into the '60s by lunch time. Hanging the "closed" sign on the door, she locked up and headed over to the building that served as city hall. The mayor was at his desk and rose as she entered.

"Hi. I'm the new librarian, Julie Lindstrom," she reminded him.

"Yes. I hope you are settling in okay. What can I do for you?"

"This sounds a little odd, I know, but actually I was wondering if you knew anything about children going missing in the woods here."

"No! Not at all." He held a smile, but his gaze shifted slightly. "Where did you hear such a thing?"

"My daughter came home from school with the story."

"Kids! Never know what they're going to make up. It was probably just an attempt to scare the 'new kid' in town."

"That could be. Anyway, thanks for seeing me,"

"No problem. Drop in any time."

As she left his office, Julie felt sure he had been hiding something. Why was everyone avoiding the issue, or was there truly nothing to the rumor?

She hit the microfiche with renewed vigor when she got back to the library. In the mid-1960s, she finally found a related story.

EIGHT-YEAR OLD GIRL SEES MONSTER IN WOODS screamed the headline. The story went on to detail her fear at seeing the horrible creature and even went so far as to print a copy of the drawing she had done of it. It stood on short legs and featured a long snout and little arms with claws. Must have been a slow news day to feature a little girl's imaginative report, Julie thought. Nothing more was printed on the subject in subsequent issues. Probably the editor's little joke.

But then in the issues from the '70s, there was another incident. A six-year old boy had disappeared. His frantic parents notified the sheriff. A search of the area was immediately organized. Men trudged through the fields and surrounding woods, swinging flashlights and calling his name, but they didn't find him. The next morning, he was spotted wandering in the field, eyes wide with fear, his face streaked with tears and his clothes covered with dirt and leaves.

"A big green monster chased me," he was quoted as saying. "I hid in a hollow log and then when it was light, I ran as fast as I could out of the woods."

According to the story, he was deeply traumatized and just kept repeating that a monster was after him. When interviewed, a few other people from town admitted that they had heard weird grunting noises coming from the area during the search, but there the story ended.

Shortly thereafter there was an announcement in the paper that the Whitakers would be putting up a "Danger" sign on the town side of the woods, warning people not to go into the area. An abandoned and crumbling mine shaft was becoming more and more unstable making walking through the woods unsafe.

And then there was nothing until the late '90s.

WHITAKER CHILDREN MISSING

Julie gasped when she saw the headline. She read on to find out that they were a boy of ten and his eight-year-old sister. Almost everyone in town had joined the search party. They combed the fields outside of town and then split up in groups to cover the woods. People who were part of the search in the woods later commented that it was dead silent, no rustling of small animals, no birds singing. The only sounds were of their own footsteps and voices. Their calls went unanswered. The children were not found, and the only indication that they might have been there was the discovery of one small red tennis shoe. The children's mother, Maureen Whitaker, said their daughter had similar shoes and it was the correct size, but otherwise it couldn't definitely be identified as hers.

Subsequent stories announced the addition of outside law enforcement agencies, alerts to nearby towns, national coverage. In an interview with a local reporter, Mrs. Whitaker made a tearful plea to anyone who could help find the children. She finished by saying that they would never have gone into the woods. They knew the danger. Her family had been the owners of the wooded area for a number of generations. She repeated, "They would not have gone into the woods."

Time passed. No sign of the children was ever forthcoming. The story faded away with an occasional mention, and then nothing.

With tears in her eyes, Julie finished the last of the reports. It had been ten years since they had gone missing. Still, why the complete denial by townspeople? Many of them had lived here then. They had to remember, especially with the Whitakers still living in the area, a constant reminder of their loss.

Julie couldn't understand it and she determined to find out the reason. Apparently the sheriff hadn't come up with anything, since she hadn't heard back from him. Who could she ask? She didn't know any of the shop owners well enough, and she didn't want to start rumors by asking the parents of Emma's schoolmates.

After a mostly sleepless night, she decided to try the real estate agent who had sold her the cottage. Since Mrs. Redmond knew her, she might be more sympathetic than the other townspeople she had talked to. After closing the library, she walked down the hill to the realtor's office. She was in luck. Lights were on inside and a neatly coiffed middle-aged woman in a business suit was seated behind one of the two desks inside.

"Mrs. Redmond?" Julie closed the door behind her as she entered.

"Yes." The woman looked up from a stack of papers on her desk.

"I was wondering if you could help me answer a few questions."

"Oh, hi, Julie, isn't it? The new librarian? How are you getting on, and what can I help you with?"

"I was doing a little research and came across a newspaper story about two children missing from the area in the '90s."

After a pause, the realtor sighed. "So sad. The poor Whitakers. The children were never found, you know."

"I know. What I was wondering was why everyone in town denies that it ever happened."

"Oh, that. I probably shouldn't be saying anything either, but since you already know about it, I don't see how it could hurt. In the '60s and '70s, because of a couple of news reports, we got a reputation as being the town with a dragon in the woods. All as a result of a misguided article in the newspaper featuring a drawing by an impressionable child. Big joke! People laughed, but still they shied away from coming here. In fact, some of the people with small children moved out. Business declined, houses stood empty. We were a dying community."

"Surely after time had passed, people forgot about it," Julie remarked.

"You're right. They mostly did and things began to pick back up. But then in 1996 or '97, can't remember which, the Whitaker kids disappeared. It was no longer a joke, it was a disaster. At one point, I didn't think any of the businesses would survive. Now we are in a comeback mode. A small, crime-free community. A healthy environment for children. We don't want a repeat of that whole 'dragon living in the woods' story. It's ridiculous, really. There's no such thing as a dragon, we all know that. If anything is in there, it's a bear or a mountain lion. The children's disappearance was just an isolated incident anyway. Maybe they fell into the mine shaft, but whatever, it was a long time ago and best forgotten."

"I see," Julie said, appalled by the woman's callous attitude. But the next thought that came to mind was whether or not she would be able to sell her house if she found a job in another town. She didn't believe in dragons, of course, but still….

Some weeks later, the door to the library opened and a tall, thin woman walked in, gazing around the room until her eyes fell on Julie. She walked hesitantly up and cleared her throat.

"Hi, I'm Dorothy Vandecar. I just moved here with my family a few weeks ago."

"Nice to meet you. Did you want a library card?"

"Well, yes, I guess so."

As she was filling out the form which Julie handed to her, Dorothy asked, "I know this sounds odd, but my kids came home from school with some tale about children going missing in those woods outside of town. Have you ever heard anything like that?"

Julie looked up at her and took the form she had finished filling out. She entered the data into the computer and printed out a library card. At the same time, she said in an offhand manner, "No. I don't think I ever heard of any missing children, though there is a dangerous mine shaft somewhere in there. There's a sign posted that the place is off limits. It's not a safe place for kids." She smiled up at the woman. "Here's your library card, Mrs. Vandecar. Welcome to Lost Pines."

FLOWERS FOR EVERY OCCASION

Stepping back, Jeannie hummed a little tune and admired her work. The flower arrangement was perfect for the occasion, snapdragons for color, baby's breath for softness. After all, only the best for this funeral. It was one she had been looking forward to. She smiled at the thought of how different her life would soon become.

Although she was called upon to provide flowers for most of the funerals held in town, she also provided love in the form of red roses and pink carnations. It was to her small shop that the town of Smithfield turned on Valentine's Day and anniversaries. She was happy that the beautiful blooms she artfully arranged enhanced so many events in their little town.

It was on just such an occasion that she first met Daniel Warner. He was running for State Assembly, and she recognized him from his pictures in the paper. He was much more handsome in person, tall with rugged features and unruly dark hair, a crooked grin lighting his face as he rushed into the shop.

"Help," he blurted. "I need roses or something. My wife is mad at me because I forgot her birthday."

"Don't worry," Jeannie said with a wink. "I'll make you an arrangement that will get her to forgive you anything."

"Oh, and can you put in some of those snapdragons?" He pointed at the vase in the cooler. "They're her favorite flower."

The finished bouquet was a work of art, really. So beautiful she wished someone had bought it for her. Not that anyone would send her flowers. Besides being ridiculous, there wasn't anyone who cared enough to do so. Because of her thick glasses and dumpy figure, few men were interested in her. All her life, she had arranged flowers for other people, of no more interest to her customers than the service she provided.

As she handed the flowers to Daniel, their hands touched and she felt an electric shock run through her. She looked up into his eyes and knew that he was the man for her. It was no accident that he had come into her shop. They were meant to be together.

"That will be $35.00." Her voice came out slightly choked, and her pulse raced.

He gave her a credit card. "I can't thank you enough. It's beautiful."

"I'm glad you like it." She ran the card through the machine, "Please sign here. Would you like to add your address to my email list? Oh, and good luck with your wife."

"Thanks. These flowers will really help." He flashed an infectious smile as he wrote his name and address on the pad she kept by the cash register.

Her heart gave a little leap when he smiled. She knew that she had finally met "the one."

He returned the next day. "I just wanted you to know that your flowers worked wonders."

Jeannie knew it was just an excuse to see her again. He had really come back because he was as drawn to her as she was to him. The previous evening she had driven by his house. It was a well-kept, two-story colonial in the better part of town. Her dream house. Just another sign that he was the man destiny had intended for her.

She gave him a flirtatious smile. "I'm so glad. We aim to please."

"I'll keep that in mind," he said as he exited the shop, the little bell signaling a new phase in her life.

For the next month, every time someone entered the store, she looked up in anticipation at the thought that it might be him. Her shoulders slumped when she saw that it was just another customer. She began to worry at the amount of time that had gone by, but she had faith that he would find a way to come back to her.

One day she found a picture of Daniel's wife, Laura, in the newspaper. Laura was hosting a charity function and was just as Jeannie had pictured her. Perfectly groomed and arrogant, helping out the less fortunate to make herself look better. *What a phony*, she thought. The article listed a number for ticket sales and Jeannie decided to attend. She wanted to get a better look at the woman who stood between her and the happiness she deserved.

The day of the luncheon, Jeannie left the shop to her part-time employee. She picked out her best black sheath, designed to give the wearer a slimmer profile. She pulled on a tight pair of panty hose, pressed the skirt down over her hips and sucked in her stomach. The addition of a pair of three-inch heels gave the impression of a svelte rather than an overly plump woman.

An hour later, she tottered into the hotel lobby on the unfamiliar high heels and followed the signs to the gala function. Once she had found her seat, she gazed around and spotted Laura Warner seated in the middle of the head table. She was smiling at the women who were coming up to her, nodding her head to acknowledge praise for staging such a successful event.

Jeannie could barely contain herself watching all the people fawning around Laura. *Smile now, you conceited bitch. It won't be long before Daniel and I are living happily in that perfect house. He'll be so much better off without you.*

The woman seated next to her broke into her thoughts. "Isn't this chocolate peanut cheesecake divine?"

"It certainly is delicious," Jeannie agreed.

"Poor Laura will never know what she missed."

"What do you mean?"

"Oh, didn't you know? She's highly allergic to peanuts. Exposure to them can cause her throat to close up. Has to carry one of those EpiPen thingies all the time." The woman looked pleased to be able to impart such inside information.

"Oh. Sorry to hear that," Jeannie said, not that she was really sorry, of course. "I'm surprised that they served it then."

"It's a house specialty so they sort of had to. But I understand the head table all got strawberry cheesecake."

Days passed and there was no sign of Daniel in her little shop. Still, she rationalized that it wouldn't do for him to look too eager. They were destined to be together. He'd be back, she was sure.

And, a week later, he did come striding through her door.

"Hi. I'd like to order some flowers." She noticed he was pretending not to remember the instant connection they had made on his first visit.

"Certainly," she said, playing along. "What's the occasion?"

"It's my fifth wedding anniversary. I want something really special."

Jeannie showed him pictures of various arrangements, all the while feeling sorry for him. Five years he had endured marriage to that woman.

"I like this one." He pointed to a particularly ornate display.

"That will take a while to put together. Do you want to come back and pick it up or have it delivered?"

"Oh. I'll pick it up."

Jeannie smiled to herself. Obviously he wanted one more opportunity to be with her.

"It will be ready at two. Are you planning a big night out?"

"Yes. I've got reservations at The Steak House."

"That sounds like fun."

"It's one of our favorite places."

"I'm sure it will be a night to remember."

"I hope so. I'll be back at two for the flowers."

He left the shop without a backward glance. He was really very discreet, she thought as she busied herself selecting the flowers. The arrangement he had chosen was a beautiful combination including roses and the obligatory snapdragons.

He returned at two as promised. Their hands touched as he handed her his credit card, and she felt the same surge of energy as before. Daniel ignored it, however. He simply took his card back, picked up the floral arrangement and walked out. He was a cool one, there was no doubt. No one would ever guess his true feelings for her. Since he was a married man, it wouldn't do to start gossip.

Jeannie read the papers and knew all about these marriages of convenience. As a budding politician, he couldn't afford to have his reputation sullied with rumors of an affair. And divorce would hamper his chances as well. She pictured herself dressed in an elegant suit, standing proudly beside him as he accepted his new position.

There was only one problem. His wife.

She knew he would do nothing to rid himself of her. As much as he wanted to be with Jeannie, he wouldn't attempt anything that might endanger his chances at election. It was up to her to find a way for them to be together.

That evening Jeannie dressed in nondescript dark clothes, stopped by the supermarket for a few things and then entered The Steak House by the door into the bar. A quick glance told her that the place was practically empty on this Monday evening. She could see Daniel and Laura sitting at one of the tables in the sparsely occupied dining area, smiling up at a waiter as they ordered.

The bartender was busy polishing glasses with his back to the door so Jeannie was able to slip quietly through the bar unseen. She turned into a narrow hall and entered the ladies room. Glad to see it was an upscale place with a comfortable chair and table in the entryway, she sank into the chair and prepared to wait. She knew it might be some time before Laura came in, but she was pretty sure that at some point in the evening, she would.

The waiting seemed interminable. A couple of times women entered, and Jeannie busied herself looking down into her purse as if she were searching for makeup.

Finally, Laura came through the door. She entered one of the stalls and Jeannie sprang into action. She quickly donned the dishwashing gloves she had bought and ripped open a big bag of peanuts. As Laura exited the stall, Jeannie pretended to stumble and threw the contents of the bag on her.

"Oh, I'm so sorry. How clumsy of me. Let me help you get the crumbs off of you." She began brushing the peanut dust into the air around Laura.

"Peanuts," Laura gasped. "Allergic. Need EpiPen." She began to rummage in her purse, obviously looking for it. She began to choke and grasped her throat, dropping the purse.

"Oh, my gosh. Here, let me help you." Jeannie grabbed the purse and dumped out its contents. At the same time, she palmed the EpiPen and rolled it into one of the stalls. "I can't find it. I'll go get help."

Laura appeared to be unconscious so Jeannie silently left the ladies room, skirted through the bar and left the restaurant. If no one came into the restroom in the next few minutes, Laura would be dead. If she did survive, all she would remember was an unremarkable but clumsy woman who had meant her no harm and who had apparently fled rather than admit responsibility. Then Jeannie would have to think of some other way to be rid of her rival. But if she were lucky …

The next morning when she picked up her morning paper, she saw that she was lucky indeed. The headline was spread across the top of the paper.

LAURA WARNER, WIFE OF STATE ASSEMBLY CANDIDATE DANIEL WARNER, DEAD IN FREAK ACCIDENT

The story went on to say that Mrs. Warner was discovered dead of anaphylactic shock in the ladies room of The Steak House where she had gone with her husband to celebrate their wedding anniversary. A broken bag of peanuts was found on the floor next to her. No one knew how it got there, and there were no identifying prints or marks on it. Since she was severely allergic to peanuts, the allergy was determined to be the cause of her death. Her EpiPen was found against the wall in one of the stalls where it had probably rolled out of her handbag while she was frantically trying to find it. Mr. Warner issued a short statement saying he was absolutely devastated by her death. One minute they were happily celebrating their anniversary and the next she was dead. He asked that his privacy be respected during this incredibly difficult time. The funeral would be held, etc….

Jeannie sighed with relief. It was done. Now all she had to do was wait for Daniel to come for her.

A secondary benefit to Laura's death turned out to be a big increase in orders for floral arrangements for the funeral. Busy filling orders, Jeannie had no time to think about the past or the future.

But time passed slowly after the rush of business brought by the funeral. She knew Daniel wouldn't come right away. After all, he had to pretend to be in mourning. Still, she would have been happier if she had heard something from him.

Finally after a long month of waiting, the bell jingled and when she looked up he was there.

"Daniel, you're here."

"Uh, hi, uh."

"Jeannie."

"Right, Jeannie. I wanted to order some flowers."

Jeannie was a little taken aback at this, but then she realized that he couldn't just come in without an excuse so soon after his wife died.

"Certainly. What did you have in mind?"

"I'd like a really pretty arrangement but not too ostentatious. Maybe some daisies and a few rosebuds."

Jeannie looked at the containers of flowers in the refrigerated case and gave a little shudder. Behind the roses, stood a vase of snapdragons, each row of little faces looking at her with menace. As if they knew what she had done. *Really, her imagination was working over time.*

"And did you want it delivered?" she asked, shaking off a dizzy spell.

"Yes. To Miss Penny Singleton at the Dorcas Apartments. Apartment 20B. You know where they're located on Gibson?"

Jeannie wondered who this Penny Singleton was, maybe one of his campaign volunteers? That was probably it. Probably her birthday or something. Just another example of how thoughtful he was.

"Of course. No problem."

"Oh. And do you have any of those little cards to put in the flowers?"

"Right here." She indicated a small rack of cards and envelopes on the counter.

He picked out a card and wrote hastily on it, then put it in one of the envelopes and handed it to her.

"Thanks so much," he said as he paid her. "See you next time."

There, she knew he would give her a hint as to what he was feeling. She picked up the little envelope and saw that he hadn't sealed it. Curious, she pulled the card out and read.

Darling Penny,

Please be patient. Now that Laura is gone we can be together always. We just have to wait a little longer.

I love you,

Daniel

A BLANK CANVAS

The small pencil sketch of a dragon hung partially hidden among the other art works in the gallery. Large colorful oil paintings overshadowed the small framed drawing, placed as almost an afterthought in one corner. The square paper next to it said "anonymous", the price was a modest $100, and there was no red dot indicating a sale.

In an effort to avoid the noisy crowd at the gallery opening, Linda had retired to an obscure corner away from the wine and snacks. Sipping her glass of Chardonnay, she was examining the works of art hanging near her when she discovered the small drawing.

Looking up, she saw her husband Geoff wending his way through the crowd while balancing a small plate of hors d'oeuvre and his wine glass. When he reached her, she snatched a cracker covered with brie from the plate and stuffed it into her mouth.

"I'm famished," she said. "We should have gone to dinner before coming to this show. I thought there'd be less people and more food."

"I know. I've looked at most of the paintings. We should cut out." Geoff washed down a cracker with a gulp of the wine.

"Look at this drawing, Geoff." Linda pointed to the dragon.

"It's nice."

"I think I'll buy it. It's only a hundred dollars and something about it really attracts me."

"Can if you want. Do you have a place for it in the apartment?"

"I'll find a place. Now how do I get the gallery owner's attention?" She looked around the room and spied him gesticulating in front of a particularly large abstract oil painting. "There he is. I'll go tell him."

When she got closer, she caught the words … "wonderful investment." The couple he was talking to were nodding and smiling.

"I hate to interrupt you, Max," Linda said, "but I'd like to purchase that small drawing of a dragon over in the corner. Do you know anything about it?"

"Not really. I found it in with a stack of paintings when I was hanging the show. I asked the artist if it was his, but he said 'no'. Had never seen it before. I saw that small space open and on a whim, hung it there. It *is* nicely rendered."

Linda took out her checkbook and started writing a check. "It's a hundred dollars plus tax?"

"Right. Let me get you a receipt." Max wrote up the sale and then handed her a small red dot. "If you don't mind, could you put this on the tag? I see some people I need to talk to."

With that, he rushed off.

Linda returned to Geoff. "Well, I own it. We can pick it up after the opening is over."

"Great. Now let's get out of here and find some food."

A few days later, Linda stopped by the gallery and picked up the drawing.

"Was your opening a success?" she asked.

"The best I've ever had. We sold almost everything," Max answered. He went in the backroom and brought back a small picture. "This is it, right?"

"Right. Did you find out anything more about where it came from?"

"No, nothing. Let me wrap it up for you." He covered it with brown paper and handed it to her. "It's a good choice though. Excellent work."

She picked up the package and left for home. Once there, she found a perfect place for it in the hall and hung it. Every day as she passed, she would stop to admire the beautiful work that had gone into it.

About a week later, she returned home from a doctor's appointment and waited anxiously for her husband to arrive. When she heard the door close, she rushed to meet him.

"Geoff! Good news."

"Good news?"

"Yes. Doctor Jamison says I'm pregnant. After all our trying, we're finally going to have a baby."

"Linda, that's great!" Geoff lifted her off her feet and swung her around. "Oh, maybe I should be more careful." He set her back down gently.

"Don't worry about it. He says I'm healthy and should carry to full term. Is this great or what? I'd better start fixing up the spare room."

Geoff laughed. "That's just like you. Can't resist a chance to redecorate. Have fun."

The following week, Linda was walking down the hall when she noticed that the dragon picture was gone. The frame now held nothing but a blank piece of paper. She pointed it out to Geoff and no matter how many theories they came up with, they couldn't figure it out.

It couldn't be theft because the paper it had been printed on was still there. After puzzling over it for a couple weeks, they settled on disappearing ink, though Linda swore the picture had been in pencil.

Of no use to them, the framed piece of paper went into the Goodwill box, and they soon forgot about it in the excitement of the approaching birth of their child.

Maggie was sifting through a box of framed pictures at the Goodwill.

"Beth, look at this." She held up the drawing of a dragon. "Isn't it beautiful?"

"It's nice. I'm not sure I like dragons," Beth said.

"Oh, but they're supposed to be good luck. And it's only three dollars. I'm getting it."

"Whatever. Did you see the sweaters? There's a lot of really nice ones on the rack."

When they were done looking through the clothes, they headed up to the counter. Beth plunked down three tops and Maggie followed, paying for her picture.

That evening, John trudged into the front door as Maggie was fixing a small meal in their crowded trailer.

"No luck, finding a job?" she asked.

"Nope. I think looking for work is harder than actually working." He sank onto the bench that served as seating for the built-in table.

"I know." Maggie gave him a kiss and set a plate in front him. "Eat it while it's hot."

"Thanks, sweetie. What did you do today?"

"Oh, nothing. Went to the thrift store with Beth."

"Buy anything?"

"Just a little picture of a dragon."

"A picture of a dragon? What on earth?"

"I'm sorry, it just wouldn't let me leave it there. I can't explain it. Anyway, it was marked three dollars, but it was a discount day so I got it for a dollar. I put it there on the counter." She pointed to the framed drawing.

"Oh, well. Only a dollar. You deserve a treat once in awhile."

A week later, John burst through the door.

"I got a job!"

"You did?"

"Yes, foreman at a paper plant. Good pay. We should be able to pay our debts and move out of this trailer."

"John. That's wonderful!" Maggie hugged him.

It wasn't long before they were able to make plans to move into an apartment nearby. While she was packing up, Maggie noticed the small frame that had been obscured by a coffee pot on the crowded counter. The picture was no longer there, just a blank piece of paper surrounded by the cheap wooden frame. She couldn't imagine what had happened to it. Maybe John hadn't liked it, but he hadn't said anything. In the excitement of the move, she shrugged it off. She took the frame and set it outside next to the trash can.

Tom Walker was making his usual rounds with the big noisy truck, picking up city trash. When he saw the beautiful dragon drawing leaning against a garbage can, he thought it was too nice to throw away. He picked it up and put it on the seat in the truck's cab and continued on his route.

That evening, he walked into his cramped little house with it in his hand.

"What's that you have?" his wife, Meredith, asked.

"Oh, it's just a picture someone threw away. It's too nice to go to the dump so I brought it home. I thought Natalie might like to see it."

Meredith glanced at it and agreed. "Since she's so serious about an art career, I'm sure she will."

"Where are the kids, anyway?"

"All four of them have gone off as usual. Natalie has a late art class at the college, both boys went to soccer practice, and Candy is at ballet class. It's just us for an hour or so."

"I could use the break," Tom said.

"Me, too. This little house is just too small for so many people. It seems no matter how hard we work, we never get ahead."

"I'm sorry I'm not a better bread winner," Tom said.

"No, no. I didn't mean that. You work really hard to provide for us, and we've been lucky enough to see our oldest get into college. It's just that the cost of everything keeps going up, and we don't seem able to put away anything towards a bigger house. By the time we can afford to move, we won't need to. We'll be wanting to downsize!" Meredith laughed.

Tom settled down on the sofa and clicked on the television while Maureen went back into the kitchen to prepare dinner.

Two weeks later, when Tom drove up in front of his house after work, Maureen rushed out to meet him.

"What's happened? Are the kids all right?" he asked in alarm.

"Yes, they're fine. It's good news!"

"What?"

"You know how you always make fun of me for buying a lottery ticket every week?"

"Yes."

"Well, we won!"

"We won?" Tom couldn't quite take it in. "We won one of the hundred dollar prizes? We can really use it. Natalie's tuition is coming due soon."

"Not a hundred dollars."

"Oh, not that much?" His voice dropped in disappointment.

"No, not that much. More! We won a million dollars!" Meredith hugged her husband. "We're rich. We can move to a bigger place, put away money for the boys and Megan to go to college. I can't believe it."

"I can't believe it either. Why didn't you call me?"

"Your cell phone is dead as usual. I couldn't wait for you to get home so I could tell you."

Once they received the check, they found a perfect house in a nice neighborhood and began packing up their things to move. Meredith found a framed piece of blank paper leaning against their sofa. She couldn't imagine where it had come from, but figured it was probably something Natalie planned to work on. She packed it up in a box with the rest of the art supplies and paintings that cluttered her daughter's room. And there it remained.

FORBIDDEN CITY

The neon dragon blinked red and yellow on the sign for the Forbidden City Chinese Restaurant. In spite of the lights shining on the black asphalt, the parking lot had an empty forsaken feel. The cleaning establishment and the nail salon flanking the restaurant were both closed and there was only one car parked in front of the restaurant, although it was after 6 p.m.

Christy looked around the lot, hesitant to get out of her car and approach the big red double doors. It was a lonely spot, and there was no sign of her friend, Meg, who had insisted she meet her at the restaurant precisely at six. But it was cold in the car so she pushed open the door and pulled herself out, straightening the jacket of her business suit as she stood. The sound of her high heels echoed in the silence as she hurried up to the entrance.

Warm air with a scent of exotic spices greeted her as she opened the door. Inside, an intricately carved screen stood behind a reception desk, shielding the eating area. An Asian woman dressed in a black blouse and black slacks smiled at her.

"One for dinner?"

"No, I'm being joined by someone."

"Would you like to wait or would you rather be seated?"

"I'll go ahead and be seated. Thanks."

"Right this way." The hostess picked up two menus and led the way around the screen.

The room was narrow with several tables draped in white on each side of an aisle. There were no other diners. Perhaps the car out front belonged to one of the employees who parked there to make the place look busy.

"Can I get you anything to drink?" the hostess asked.

"Just some tea, please," Christy said.

"Of course." The woman headed towards the kitchen in the back and returned quickly with a pot of tea. "You might want to let it steep for a few minutes."

Then she went up front, leaving Christy alone in the room.

After about a fifteen minute wait, with Christy getting ever more impatient, an elderly woman came out from a kitchen in the back, bowed slightly and asked if she would like a bowl of soup and egg rolls.

"I think that would be perfect. My friend seems to have been delayed."

The soup and egg rolls arrived. Christy was hungry and the food was delicious, but still no Meg. After a half hour, she checked her phone but there were no messages. Ordinarily she wouldn't use her phone in a restaurant, but since she was alone in the room, she tried dialing Meg. The call went straight to voicemail. Thoroughly annoyed by now, Christy pushed her dishes away. The woman returned from the back and asked if she would like anything else, but Christy declined, anxious to get on her way home. She waited another fifteen minutes and then rose and went to the front.

"I'm sorry. My friend doesn't seem to be coming. Could you give me my check and if she does show up, tell her I couldn't wait any longer?"

"Certainly."

The hostess handed her the bill on a tray along with the customary fortune cookie.

Christy unwrapped the cookie, broke it in half and pulled out the thin slip of paper.

"Beware of friends who wear false faces."

Wow, she thought to herself. *That's an odd fortune.*

She picked up her purse and as she was paying her bill, a group of young people entered. She pushed through the small crowd and rushed to her car, glad that business seemed to be picking up for the place, but annoyed at the time she had wasted sitting there.

Darn that Meg anyway. What was she thinking – standing me up like this?

As Christy drove home, she reviewed her conversation with Meg. The phone had rung in her plush office at the Evans Advertising Agency where she worked. Since her secretary had the day off, she'd looked at the caller ID and picked up the phone.

"Hi, Meg, what's up?"

"I have to talk to you," Meg had said. "Can you meet me at the Forbidden City Chinese Restaurant on First Street at six?"

"I guess. Sounds urgent."

"It's exciting news. Just have to share. Tell you about it when I see you. Be sure to be there at six. Bye now."

And that had been that. A childhood friend, Meg had not been as successful as Christy. In order to make a living, she had been forced to work both as a waitress and occasional stints as an office temp. She had even worked at Evans for a week or so. It had been a little awkward, so Christy had just treated her like one of the other employees. She hadn't wanted to look too chummy, but ever since then, their relationship had been a little strained. Still, they continued to meet for the occasional lunch

Christy thought Meg might be resentful of her success, but if she was, she hid it well. Neither of them had been married, though Christy had been engaged to Dylan, a coworker at the advertising agency, for a time. Christy's upward rise in the company plus her ever-increasing income had come between them. Now when they passed in the hallways, they both managed a perfunctory nod in acknowledgement, but it was obvious that Dylan resented her seniority while he still toiled as an assistant in one of the other departments.

Still thinking about the missed meeting, Christy pulled into the carport assigned to her condominium, killed the motor and gathered her purse and briefcase.

What could have been so urgent? And then not urgent enough to show up at the appointed time?

As she went to unlock her door, she saw that it was ajar. She pushed it open and gasped in horror.

The entire room was a shambles. Books pulled off shelves, cushions ripped, drawers emptied.

Fearful that someone might still be in the house, she backed out and called 911. When she heard the "whup, whup" of sirens as the police car drove up, she rushed to meet it. Two uniformed men were stepping from the car as she approached.

"Hi," she gasped. "It was me that called. When I opened the door to my place, I saw that there had been intruders. I ran, in case they might still be in the building."

"You did the right thing, Miss," one of the officers said. "Let us go in first."

The officers approached the open door, guns drawn, and entered, sweeping the room with their eyes. Once they had ascertained that there was no one there, they checked the closets and the two back bedrooms. The condominium was empty.

"There's no one in here, Miss," one called to Christy. "It's safe to come in. It looks like a burglary or maybe just vandalism. Can you tell, has anything been stolen?"

"I don't see anything gone."

She moved into the bedroom, and although things were strewn everywhere, she could see that the obvious items seemed to still be there.

"No. The TV and computer are here." A quick glance into her jewelry box showed no evidence of anything missing. "All my jewelry seems to be here as well."

"Well, it appears to be a random act unless you know that someone has it in for you. Are you aware of any such person?"

"No, no. I don't know of anyone who would want to victimize me."

"Well, then come down to the station tomorrow and file a report. And, oh, make sure you call a locksmith. Whoever did this obviously had no trouble picking the lock."

"I will. Thank you so much for coming," Christy said, closing the door behind them.

Surveying the mess, she slumped into a chair. She had no clue as to where to start. Since she had to go to work in the morning, she headed into the bedroom. She picked up the clothes that had been emptied from the bedroom drawers, hung up the clothes from the closet and examined her jewelry case. Everything was there except a pair of pearl earrings in a trademark blue Tiffany box that her mother had left her. At first she thought it was just in the jumble of stuff on the floor, but no matter how she searched, the box didn't turn up.

The next morning she called to say she would be late to work and then waited for the locksmith and cleaning service to arrive.

After all the details had been taken care of, she headed out to her car, a silver BMW, her prize possession, intending to stop by the police station to sign the obligatory report. But another unpleasant surprise awaited her. All four tires had been punctured.

Another two hours were lost getting the car back into operation. The gas tank had also been drained. Finally, she made it into the office.

"Mr. Evans asked that you come to his office when you get in." Her secretary didn't look up from the paperwork in front of her as Christy plunked her briefcase onto her desktop.

She took a deep breath and made her way down the corridor to the big office at the end. Ted Evans sat frowning behind the old antique desk that dominated the room.

"Have a seat, Christy."

"You would not believe the day I've had," Christy said as she took the seat opposite her boss. "I'm sorry I got into work so late, but my house was ransacked and my car was vandalized."

"This is not about your late arrival, Christy," Evans said. "I'm sorry to say this, and I can hardly believe it, but it has come to my attention that you have been planning to start your own agency and have been trying to recruit our clients."

"What? But, no! There's no truth to that. I've never been interested in starting my own agency. I like it here."

"I would like to believe that, but I have here a copy of the letter you sent out, on our letterhead I might add, to one of our clients. It states unequivocally that that is your intention. I can't ignore such blatant evidence. Please pick up your severance check in accounting and remove any personal items from your office. You have fifteen minutes."

"But, Mr. Evans, I've done no such thing. Please believe me."

"The letter spells it all out quite clearly."

"Where did the letter come from?"

"It arrived in my mail anonymously this morning."

"Did you call the client?"

"Yes, he confirmed that he had received it, but he had no intention of changing agencies so hadn't mentioned it. The letter I got was a copy of the one sent to him. There were a few changes marked on it so I can only assume it was a rough draft. Probably discovered by a coworker who didn't want to get involved, hence the anonymous mailing. In any case, you are no longer welcome here."

"But, Mr. Evans, I didn't do it."

"Goodbye, Miss Marshall," he said with finality, turning to the files on his desk.

Having no recourse, Christy picked up the check, boxed up her things and left the building. As she passed her secretary, the woman refused to meet her eyes, and the halls seemed strangely empty, everyone apparently avoiding the train wreck that had just occurred.

Christy couldn't believe this was happening. Still, she knew she was good at what she did. She would find another job.

Back home, she dismissed the cleaners, figuring to save money and finish the job herself, but once they were gone she sank into a chair and buried her face in her hands.

Had there ever been a worse twenty-four hours in her life?

After awhile, she stood, went into the kitchen, mixed herself a drink, and called Meg.

"Hi, Christy, so sorry I stood you up last night," Meg blurted when she picked up. "My car wouldn't start, and the battery on my phone was dead."

"That's not why I called. I just had to talk to someone. I have had the most awful run of bad luck." With all that had gone on, Christy had forgotten that Meg had wanted to talk about something important. "Wait, what did you want to see me about?"

"Oh, I wanted to tell you I think I'm actually seeing someone serious."

"Wow. That's great. Who is it?"

"Never mind that now. What's happened?"

"When I got home, I found my house vandalized. And then my tires were punctured. I was late to work, and when I got there I found that someone had made unfounded charges against me and I was fired."

"What? But that's ridiculous."

"I know, but I couldn't prove I hadn't done what they said. Do you want to meet for a drink or something?"

"I'm so sorry, but I can't tonight. I'm working. How about lunch tomorrow?"

"That would be great. You're a lifesaver, Meg."

"OK. See you at Dante's at noon?"

"Terrific."

It was really nice to have a girlfriend to confide in, Christy thought as she entered the restaurant. She didn't have much of a support system, her parents were dead and she had no siblings, so it was pretty much Meg plus a few other friends from school. She spied Meg waving at her from a nearby table and wove her way over. Meg immediately stood and hugged her.

"I'm so sorry about all your bad news. Let's just have a martini and try to forget about it. What will you do now?" she said, immediately contradicting herself.

"I'm going to go out and look for another job. After all, I am experienced and should have great references from my clients."

"Well, there you are. Let me know if I can help in any way." Meg smiled at her, and they picked up their menus to order.

"But what about you? Who is this new guy?"

"Oh, just someone I met at one of my temp jobs. Compared to your problems, it's not that important. I'm just hoping it works out."

Christy lifted her glass and said, "Here's to both our new ventures."

"To a better future." Meg clinked her glass.

As it turned out, getting another job wasn't as easy as Christy expected. It was a small community, and the word was out. She had tried to cheat her former employer. Everywhere she turned, she was told "No." Moving away would be the only option, but even as she sent out resumes, she knew she would be unable to get the good references she would need. As expected, she received no job offers from her inquiries.

Christy called Meg. "I'm sorry to keep leaning on you, but my savings are getting low. I was wondering if you knew of any part-time work I might get."

"I can hook you up with a temp agency, and I know of a couple of restaurants that sometimes need waitresses."

"Thanks, Meg. You're a lifesaver."

She had also signed up for a few classes at the local junior college, hoping to change careers. However, her new schedule of part-time jobs interfered with her attendance, and she was too tired at night to study. She eventually dropped out. She was a total failure as a waitress, klutzy and inefficient. She had to give Meg credit, it was harder than it looked. Soon she could no longer find a restaurant that would hire her.

With fewer and fewer jobs available, Christy couldn't make ends meet. Credit card bills still came in from purchases she had made while working at the agency. Her condominium was repossessed. She had to sell her BMW and buy a second hand clunker. She found a small apartment in a lower rent part of town and scraped together enough money to buy food and gas. Her appearance had also suffered. Her once neatly-styled black hair now looked lank and disheveled, her beautiful manicured nails were cut short and dabbed with dollar store polish. She had even begun to gain weight due to a too-frequent diet of fast food.

Once word got out about her situation, she found that most of the women she had thought of as friends were no longer interested in maintaining contact. *Friends with false faces as in her fortune cookie prediction?* Through all this, her one steadfast friend remained Meg. Christy didn't know what she would have done without her.

A year passed, one day after another with no hope in sight. Christy grew more and more exhausted, more and more depressed. The day came when she could no longer bear the endless drudgery. With no prospect for a brighter future and unable to face years of hand to mouth existence, she walked to the bridge over the river that ran through town, looked down into the roiling, gray waters and escaped into them.

Meg smiled up at her fiancé, Dylan, as she carefully extracted a pearl earring from a Tiffany box on her dresser and began fastening one in her ear.

"I'm so happy about your promotion at the advertising agency, darling. Now we can begin to improve our lifestyle. I know of a repossessed condominium that's up for sale at a really reasonable price. What do you think?"

THE CAROUSEL

The intricately-carved, garishly painted animals rose and fell in time to the organ music. Horses, their necks arched, tails streaming behind them circled in a race they could never win. Tigers, giraffes and even two beautiful green dragons, their open mouths seemingly ready to breathe fire at any moment, joined the endless circuit.

"Mommy, I want to ride the dragon," Billy cried.

"All right. Wait until it stops. I'll lift you up."

The little boy jumped up and down anxiously as the ride slowly wound to a halt.

"Just a minute, Ma'am," the attendant said as she handed him a ticket. "I'll help you."

"Thanks so much. He's getting a little heavy for me to lift. It's his birthday today, and he's been so excited about coming here."

"The little boys all want to ride the dragons, it seems. Little girls, now, they prefer the horses."

Then the machinery started up and the merry-go-round began to slowly build up speed. Billy's mother stood and watched as her tow-headed child hung on tightly to the vertical pole, face frozen in a combination of fear and delight. She smiled to herself, remembering when she was little and the most exciting ride at the amusement park wasn't the roller coaster but the carousel.

She waved at him as he passed by again. He smiled, but he was afraid to let even one hand loose so that he could wave back.

The next time a dragon went by, there was no rider. She figured she had just lost track of how far it had gone around and waited, but the next dragon also held no rider.

Suddenly panicked, she rushed to the attendant.

"Stop the ride! My little boy must have fallen off. I can't see him. He was on a dragon and now he's not there."

"Oh, my gosh!" The man pulled on the brakes.

Slowly the carousel ground to a halt, and they both rushed onto the ride, but there was no sign of Billy. He wasn't on any of the animals or on the wooden platform or in the middle near the machinery. Calling his name, his mother dodged in and out between the animals looking frantically for her son. He was nowhere to be seen.

The police were called. They took statements, sent out an Amber alert and began a thorough search of the entire amusement park. They came up empty, however, and the distraught mother was eventually forced to return to her home without her son. The incident was front page news the next day. Flyers were printed and posted everywhere. A reward was offered, and people undertook searches of the area. Still, days went by and then months. Billy had disappeared without a trace.

Bill Stalling rolled over in his bed and cracked one eye at the clock. Six a.m. He really hated these early mornings, but he dragged himself up, swung his feet to the floor and stumbled bleary-eyed into the bathroom. It was his twenty-first birthday, but it was just another day like all the others in this place. He had grown up to be a little over six feet, muscular from years of hard work, and his hair still glinted with touches of gold. He stared into the mirror and rubbed the stubble on his chin while he grabbed a razor. Neatness was a requirement in the compound.

A half hour later, he was showered and shaved. He gobbled down a quick breakfast of coffee and toast and headed out the door of his small cottage to join the stream of men moving slowly down the tree-lined lane. Some were gray-haired and stooped, most were young men like himself, and there were a couple of younger boys being trained to replace the older men as they became incapacitated. The young ones arrived fearful and crying, but the older men taught them their duties, and slowly they grew into their jobs. He vividly remembered his first days here and the despair that descended on him when he realized he would never see his mother again.

The dragons, two huge green monsters with flashing red eyes and dangerous whipping tails, were already up and breathing fire, waiting for the men to bring their morning meal.

"Mornin', Bill," one of the men said as he pushed a huge wheelbarrow full of food towards the nearest dragon, careful to avoid its sharp claws and fiery breath.

"Mornin." Bill began the endless job of cleaning the cave and hauling in supplies.

The word *escape* was in every man's thoughts but never voiced. Just to utter the word brought gloom and depression. It was impossible, as they all knew. Better not to even think of it, and so they lived out their days in a never-ending routine. With the exception of some of the younger men, all hope of rescue had been beaten out of them.

"Do you think there's any way we could get away from here?" Bill broached the subject to one of the men near him.

"You saw what happened to Jim when he tried to run away," the man whispered, looking over his shoulder in fright.

Bill nodded. Jim's whole right side was scarred from a terrible burn, witness to what the dragons were capable of when angered.

If only he hadn't chosen to ride the dragon on that carousel, Bill thought. He had spent years waiting on the dragons, and the rest of his life stretched ahead of him with no end in sight. He had no future, just years of servitude until he became one of the old men who lived day to day without hope or happiness. He would rather die than continue this monotonous existence.

His only chance was to kill the dragons. He just had to figure out how.

Fairy tales always showed the brave prince holding a large sword as he challenged the ferocious animal. This wouldn't work in real life, Bill knew. In the first place, even in repose, thick clouds of smoke escaped from their nostrils, spewing carbon monoxide into the air and making it impossible to get close enough to use a sword. And even if it were possible to kill one of them that way, the other would retaliate immediately, an attack Bill knew he could not survive.

No, there had to be another way.

Every day he wracked his brain trying to think of a plan to get rid of them. Poison? Because of their size, it would probably take more then he could ever acquire to even make them a little bit sick. And, judging by their diet, they could pretty much eat anything without ill effect. Guns were out of the question. There were none here, and Bill doubted that a bullet would pierce their heavy scales in any case.

They had to have a weakness. He just had to find out what it was.

Fire? Hah! They loved it. Still, a smoldering fire could kill by asphyxiation, and as they snored and snorted in their sleep, they emitted enough smoke to fill their cave. Perhaps he could block off the air vents to the cave. They could die from their own noxious fumes. This might actually work if he could figure out a way to do it. He decided to try. He had nothing to lose. If they killed him, it would only shorten the life sentence he was serving.

Luckily, as the dragons had aged, they had become hard of hearing, complacent and slow moving. At night, they slept heavily, seemingly never disturbed by the occasional thunder clap or lightning strike. Not particularly intelligent, they never suspected that any of their captive slaves would attempt to harm them, so they paid no attention to what the men did in their spare time.

Bill began to set his plan in motion. First he found some huge rocks in the hills above the compound. It was hard work, but he managed to roll them above the cave, leaving them near the air holes that ventilated the dragon's living area. He didn't ask any of the other men to help him. He knew that they no longer had the will to fight back and, in any case, he didn't want to endanger anyone else's life. It took about a month of back breaking labor, but eventually that part of his plan was completed.

Next, he surreptitiously paced off the cave's entrance to get an exact measure of the opening. He scavenged old rusty metal pieces from the compound and then spent hours each evening crafting a huge metal door to fit.

"For goodness sakes, Bill, will you hold it down?" one of his neighbors complained. "What the hell are you doing over there anyway?"

"I'm working on a metal sculpture. Have to have something to stave off boredom."

"Well, okay. But don't work so late. You're keeping me awake." He left mumbling to himself, "Artists!"

"Sorry. I'll try not to disturb you anymore." An easy promise to make, his door was all but finished.

Getting up his nerve the next night, he decided it was now or never. First, he climbed up above the cave and rolled the rocks in place. Then, using one of the earthmovers the dragons kept for repairing the damage their occasional firefights caused, he pushed the metal door into place, listening for any signs of stirring inside the cave. Loud snores met his ears. Using dirt and mortar, he filled the spaces at the edge of the door where it met the cave entrance. His stomach in turmoil, he waited anxiously for a response. None came.

Finally, he trudged back to his cottage and fell into bed. Staring at the ceiling, he lay awake, fearing the coming morning and the terrible anger of the dragons when they realized what he had done.

As the sun rose, he joined the rest of the men as they walked towards the cave, hanging well to the back of the group. Ahead of him, he heard shocked voices rising in disbelief.

"What's that metal thing?"

"What's happened?"

"Where are the dragons?"

The men stood quietly outside the cave entrance, waiting for the dragons to burst out. Minutes went by and then an hour. There was no sound from inside. The dragons failed to appear. Gradually, they realized they were free. The older men milled around aimlessly, unsure of what to do. The younger ones grabbed their belongings and left. Bill was the first to go.

Early one morning, the owner of the carousel stood looking at the ride as a tired and bedraggled young man carrying a duffle bag approached.

"Hello, young fella'," he said. "Up early, ain't you? Parks's not open yet."

"Hi. Actually I was wondering if you needed any help around here. I'm looking for a job."

"As a matter of fact, I do have a job that needs to be done. My name's Bud." The man held out his hand to shake Bill's.

"Mine is Bill. Glad to meet you."

"Well, Bill, you came at a good time. I need someone to help me replace these two old wooden dragons with a couple of restored horses I just acquired. The dragons have been here a good long time, but just recently they started looking worn and faded, pieces are even falling off. It's time they're retired."

"I'd be happy to help," Bill said with a smile.

A GOOD LUCK CHARM

Black clouds scudded across a darkening sky as Sarah approached her local grocery store. Trailed by her six year old daughter, Olivia, who had insisted on helping Mommy with the shopping, she mentally reviewed her grocery list while she picked her way across the parking lot.

"Mommy, Mommy. What's that?" Olivia said, pointing to a pinprick of multi-hued light ahead of her.

The light flickered and then disappeared.

"I don't know, honey. It's nothing."

"No, Mommy, it looks pretty. Maybe it's a magic bean." Her daughter, currently enamored of everything described in her storybooks, ran ahead of her towards the spot.

"Wait for me, Miss." Sarah stepped up her pace.

Another bright gleam pierced the darkness and then dimmed, leaving only a glint of silver against the black asphalt.

Sarah squinted in the half light and spied a small charm lying next to the curb. A broken silver chain lay nearby. Olivia reached for it, but Sarah stopped her.

"Don't pick it up, honey. It's dirty and it looks sharp," she said, scooping up the charm. Turning it over in her hand, she could see that it was a beautifully-wrought dragon with a mesmerizing emerald-green eye, minute scales and tiny claws. Leaning over, she picked up the chain and took a quick look around the parking lot. With the exception of a few cars pulled into slots near the door, the lot was fairly empty. A few solitary individuals were hurrying towards the doors, but no one seemed to be looking at the ground as if they had lost something.

"Let me see. Let me see," Olivia begged.

"It's a good luck dragon." Sarah held it out so Olivia could see it in the light from the store windows.

Then she put it in her pocket and continued into the store. With the help of her small daughter, she managed to find everything on her list and by the time she pushed her loaded cart through the checkout line, her curious find was long since forgotten.

It was the usual morning rush the next day as her family made their departures. The kids had dawdled over their cereal and now were in danger of being late.

"Bye, hon. Have a good day," Sarah called to her husband, who was inhaling the last of his coffee while digging in his pocket for his car keys.

"Will do. You, too." He grabbed his briefcase and rushed out the door.

"Come on, you guys," she said to her two children, while wrestling them into their coats and hats. "It's time to catch the school bus."

"M-o-o-m. We're coming already." Her son shouldered his backpack and took his little sister's hand.

Sarah smiled. The routine was always the same, every morning much like every other morning. Safe and predictable.

From the doorway, she watched them run down the sidewalk to the bus stop and take their places in line. Sunlight was reflected off small puddles of water remaining on the sidewalk from the previous night's rain. The sunny morning was a welcome relief from the recent gray days.

What a perfect day for a walk, she thought. With the house empty, there was nothing to stop her from taking advantage of the good weather. Housework could wait. She grabbed her coat from the hook by the door and headed out. The last of a damp San Francisco fog was rising from the grass. Dew drops sparkled in the sun. Shoving her hands into her pockets to ward off the cool morning air, her fingers closed on a small piece of metal. She shivered from a sudden chill. The sun wasn't as warm as she had thought. She pulled her coat closed more tightly and lifted the neglected charm from her pocket for a closer inspection.

In the bright light of day, she again marveled at the dragon's artistry.

I wonder how old it is, where it came from. Maybe I should have someone look at it. It could be valuable.

As she thought about it, Chinatown seemed the logical choice for an expert opinion. Once the decision was made, she wasted no time. She ran back to the house, picked up her purse and started down the hill, quickly covering the three blocks to Market Street. It wasn't long before she heard the clatter of old metal and the familiar dinging of an approaching trolley, a bright yellow car sporting the name of the city from which it had been rescued. She boarded it, rode to Montgomery Street, exited, and headed up the hill to Grant Avenue.

The ornamental archway that marked the entrance to Chinatown also acted as a gateway to a totally foreign world hidden in the midst of this huge city. She loved the bustle of busy shoppers conversing in foreign tongues, the imposing façade of Old Saint Mary's Cathedral, the smell of exotic foods, and the carvings, silks and Asian artifacts in shop windows.

Once there, she strolled along the sidewalk, passing stores crowded with tourist souvenirs, looking for a business that might know something about the silver dragon. Her hand clasped the charm, and the sharp edges of the metal bit into her skin. Sarah shivered again and walked faster to keep warm.

In the next block, between a shop selling ducks, which hung unappetizingly from hooks in the window, and a small storefront crammed with embroidered slippers, inexpensive carvings and garish postcards of the city, she found an obviously upscale import store. Its elegant and understated windows provided a sharp contrast to the neighboring businesses. If anyone would know about her dragon, it would be a place like this. She pushed the door open and a little bell tinkled as she entered. An old man, glasses perched on his nose and wearing a traditional Chinese robe, looked up from behind a long glass case displaying silver and jade jewelry.

Perfect.

"Yes. May I help you?" He bowed slightly.

"I hope so. I found this pendant and was wondering if you could tell me anything about it." She held the charm out to him.

The man reached for it, but immediately dropped it. In fact, she thought she saw a red mark on his hand where he had grasped it.

"Did it cut you?" she asked, afraid that he might have been snagged by one of the claws.

"No, no. It is nothing. You say you found this?"

"Yes. I've heard dragons bring good luck."

"That is usually true, but I'm sorry I don't recognize this particular design. Perhaps a jeweler? I only deal in antiques, and the silver on this charm shows no sign of wear. It appears new."

This said, he scuttled around the showcase and held the door open for her. She had no choice but to leave. She heard a sharp click behind her and, turning back, she saw that he had locked his door and turned out the lights.

"Weird," she said under her breath.

Across the street was a shop with two long, red silk panels hanging in front. She strode up to the door hoping she would have better luck there. An attractive Asian woman dressed in an ornate cheongsam was behind the counter, and Sarah held the dragon charm out to her as she approached.

"Hi. I wondered if you could tell me anything about this charm I found."

The woman took it from Sarah and held it up to the light. She shook her head.

"I really can't help you. I don't know much about charms. Maybe you could research it, like on the internet?" she said, handing it back to Sarah. Then taking Sarah's arm, she ushered her out of the door.

The internet? Honestly! What happened to traditional culture? It was obviously a mistake to come here. No one seems to know anything about it, and I've been wasting my time as well as theirs. It's probably not valuable at all. Still, it's beautiful. I'll get a new chain for it and wear it – maybe find out if it's sterling. If nothing else, it will be a conversation piece.

Walking back down the hill, Sarah glanced up at the entrance to the Cathedral on the other side of the street. She loved the old building and never missed an opportunity to make a quick visit. Entering the nave, she reached her hand into the holy water font, but drew it back at once. The water was ice cold, and the tips of her fingers turned bright red. Shaken, she decided to end her tour of Chinatown and return home.

Outside, the sun had disappeared and huge dark clouds now hung low over the buildings. Thunder rumbled in the distance.

Sarah rushed down the broad, granite steps.

Funny, I don't remember any rain in the forecast. I'd better hurry if I want to keep from getting drenched.

Darting across the street, she failed to see a car turning the corner. Her piercing scream rose above the street noises as it plowed into her. She reached out to break her fall and the charm rolled out of her hand. It came to rest against the curb on the other side of the street.

Passersby, drawn by the accident scene, the bleeding woman sprawled on the street and the distant wail of an ambulance, gathered in little clusters on the sidewalk. A young woman on her lunch hour from the Financial District was attracted by a glint of silver at her feet. Leaning over, she picked up the charm and gazed in wonder at its beauty.

A good luck omen, she thought.

THE MAGICIAN'S LEI

Mary Ann strolled into the little shop behind Bubba's Burgers in Hanalei. If she hadn't sat at the counter munching on a burger and fries, she would have missed it. The small house was set back off the road and the name immediately caught her interest, Havaiki Oceanic and Tribal Art. She was attracted to art of every kind so after she finished her lunch, she climbed the wooden steps to the entrance. Once through the door, she was literally in another world. The walls were hung with art work from the many Polynesian islands. Amazing, spectacular, intricate in design, she didn't know where to look first. She edged around the rooms, peeking at sand paintings, decorated skulls, carved swords. A close look at the price tags told her she probably couldn't afford many of the items, but then she didn't know if she could choose one from the incredible selection anyway.

One room was painted black, and the only light came from spotlights on the various objects, making the vivid colors even more striking.

When she had made her way back to the counter, she smiled at the young man behind the desk.

"Thank you so much," she said. "Everything in here is wonderful. I particularly like the sand painting in the darkened room."

"I know. I love working here," the man said. "The owners sail around to all the islands collecting these amazing art pieces. Every piece is a jewel. Did you see the dragon lei?"

"No. Where is it?"

"Oh, let me show you. It's remarkable." He led her back into the darkened room and pointed out a lighted case holding three leis made of seashells. "The longer ones are for dancers. See the one in the middle. The head is a dragon shell, and the rest of it is made from shells gathered on Ni'ihau – you know, the island off Kauai where only natives are allowed. You have to have special permission to go there. An old man, living in the jungle, makes the leis from the shells his family and friends gather for him. The other name for this lei is the magician's lei."

"A magician's lei? As in magic? Could it bring me good luck?"

"I don't know, but why not?"

Mary Ann knew she had to have it. Somehow, this lei had been made especially for her. She was sure of it.

"How much is it?"

He told her and though it was way over her budget, she said, "I'll take it."

He carefully removed the necklace from its case and started to wrap it in tissue paper.

"No need to wrap it," she said. "I'll wear it."

She rationalized that she needed some magic. This trip was a treat she was giving herself to escape all her troubles. The past few months had been difficult, and she needed a break. After going with the same man for six years and with marriage her ultimate goal, she'd been devastated when he suddenly announced he had met "someone" and had unceremoniously dumped her. She had gone into a deep depression, wondering what was wrong with her. Why had he left?

Her friends tried to cheer her up. They took her for drinks after work and out for the occasional lunch or shopping trip. Mary Ann tried to join in and act like she was enjoying herself. But it was obvious that she really wasn't into it. Not to mention, she was absolutely no fun to be around. Gradually the invitations lessened, and she spent most of her evenings at home alone with the TV.

She felt her life was at an end. Here she was in her early thirties, still attractive though she was fighting a battle to stay that way. Maybe not movie star looks, but she had a trim figure, shiny black hair and dark eyes. In the old days, she'd had no trouble attracting men. But she had been out of the dating scene for too long. Every place she went, the men and women were younger. It was a different look, a different scene. She was almost over the hill in their eyes and now there was no man in her life. She was stuck in a humdrum job in Silicon Valley surrounded by computer nerds.

One day she had seen her ex walking along the street, his arm around a shapely blonde. They were laughing together, probably at one of his silly jokes. Her throat tightened, and she had to take a deep breath. She turned and went straight to the phone at her desk, called a travel agent and booked a trip to Hawaii.

Now two days into her seven day stay, she was wandering around the small Hawaiian town, going in and out of the shops, enjoying the warm air and tropical breezes. She was suffering a little buyer's remorse over the amount she had spent on the lei, but she liked the feel of the smooth shells against her skin.

Chatting with a clerk in one of the stores, she backed out the door and collided with a tall man who was entering at the same time.

"Oh, I'm so sorry," she said.

"No, no, totally my fault," he said. "I wasn't looking where I was going."

"Neither was I so I guess we're both at fault," she laughed.

"Did I hurt you?"

"Not at all." Stepping back, Mary Ann could see that not only was he tall, but very well built. A surfer, maybe? A deep tan accented his beautiful white smile, making his piercing blue eyes all the more striking. He was very well dressed for the islands, in slacks and a polo shirt. Make that a golfer, maybe?

"Well, since we've been thrown together, perhaps we should introduce ourselves. My name is David Barnard."

"I'm Mary Ann Walsh."

"Nice to meet you, Mary Ann Walsh. Are you here on vacation?"

"Yes. For the week."

"Me. too. I'm staying in a timeshare in Princeville. They have terrific golf courses there. Do you play?"

"No, not really. But I'm staying in Princeville also. Rented a condo there."

"Since we seem to be neighbors, what would you say to a neighborly drink?"

"I'd say it sounds like a great idea." Mary Ann couldn't believe it. This good looking guy was actually asking her to have a drink with him. She smoothed her fingers over the lei. Maybe it was magic after all.

He took her elbow, steering her along the sidewalk to a bar at the end of the block.

"Does this look okay?"

"Perfect."

It was early and the place was mostly empty. They pulled out two barstools and sat. The bartender wiped his hands on a towel and ambled over.

"What can I get you folks?"

"What would you like to drink?" David asked.

Mary Ann racked her brain for a drink that would seem appropriate and came up with, "Maybe a Blue Hawaiian?"

"Perfect choice. Bartender, I'll have a Cutty Sark on the rocks and the lady will have a Blue Hawaiian."

"Coming right up."

Once their drinks were served, there was an awkward little silence, and they both rushed to fill it.

"So …"

"What …"

They both laughed. After that the conversation flowed smoothly. They compared notes, found they both lived and worked in the Bay Area. Mary Ann told funny anecdotes about the computer geeks she worked with. David related stories about some of the clients he dealt with in his business as a partner in an architectural firm.

"Look at the time." David consulted his watch. "It's almost time for dinner. I hate eating alone. Would you like to join me? We could even eat here."

"I'd love to."

Dinner lasted into early evening. David picked up the check and they walked out into a beautiful sunset. Too good to be true, Mary Ann thought.

"Since we came in separate cars, I'll follow you back. Make sure you get home safely."

"Thanks. But I'm sure I'll be fine."

"Nevertheless."

He walked her to her rental car and then went to get his car. As he pulled up behind her, she noticed it was definitely an upgrade from the Dodge Avenger she was driving. She started up the motor and, when he pulled behind her, she drove out the main street, across the one lane bridge and on into Princeville. He parked next to her and walked her to the front door.

"There's a hot tub next to the pool," she said, "in case you want to indulge."

"How about dinner tomorrow night and hot tub after? I have an early tee time tomorrow morning."

"That would be terrific."

"OK. I'll pick you up here about four."

"Good night," she called as he walked away.

As soon as the door closed behind her, she twirled around, arms in the air out of pure joy. He'd asked her out for the next night. She couldn't believe her luck.

One look in the mirror and she cringed. Good grief, she had on wrinkled capris, a nondescript T-shirt, and her hair was a mess. It was a miracle he hadn't turned tail and run at the sight of her. Well, she would fix that.

The next morning she sought out a beauty salon and had the works, pedicure, manicure, facial, and hair style. By four, she was dressed in the sexiest sundress she had brought with her, amazing stilettos and, lastly, she fastened the dragon lei around her neck just as she heard his knock at the door.

"Wow. You look fantastic." He kissed her lightly on the cheek.

"Thanks."

"I thought we'd go to the Princeville Hotel for dinner, if that's all right," he said.

"Perfect." She had really wanted to go there, but it was too high end for her budget.

They walked out, got in the car and drove the winding drive to where the huge hotel hunkered on cliffs overlooking the ocean. David pulled up to the curb and handed the valet his keys. They crossed the massive lobby to the restaurant, and he gave his name to the maitre 'd.

The meal was wonderful. Mary Ann no longer felt awkward but instead was more comfortable on a date than she could ever remember being, even in her time with old what's-his-name.

On the drive back, David said that he had brought his swimsuit if she still wanted to soak in the hot tub. She certainly did.

After unlocking the door, she gestured towards the extra bedroom.

"You can use the spare room to change."

In her own room, she chose to wear the one piece bathing suit she had brought. A bikini was a little much for the occasion, she thought. Feeling uncomfortable with so much skin showing, she slid into a cover-up and walked back out into the living room. She found him clad in a boxer-type suit and Hawaiian shirt, standing on the balcony looking out over the green valley.

"The view here is amazing."

"Yes, it's gorgeous, but of course almost everything here is. Shall we?"

They walked out to the pool area and around to the hot tub. She was a little self-conscious about shedding her cover-up but, once they were in the water, she didn't give it another thought. They splashed in the shallow water, soaked in the steam, and soon she was entirely relaxed.

"Well, I'd better get going home," David said after awhile. "Another early tee time, I'm afraid."

Mary Ann was disappointed to see the evening end, but she smiled and stood, leading the way back to her condo. They went into their respective rooms to change and met in the kitchen.

"Dinner again tomorrow night?" David asked

"Absolutely."

"Is it okay to leave my suit and shirt here? We can use the hot tub again."

"No problem."

"See you tomorrow, then." But just as he was leaving, he turned and pulled her towards him. With his arms around her, he kissed her in a way that made her knees weak. "Good night."

"Good night."

When the door closed, Mary Ann just had to pinch herself. This couldn't be real, but apparently it was.

The next three nights flew by. The evenings were idyllic and at the end, the encounters more and more passionate.

"It doesn't seem possible that this wonderful week is at an end," David sighed. They were relaxing in the condo living room. He leaned back in his chair and put his feet up on the coffee table. "Luckily we live close enough so that we can still be together once we get back to the mainland."

"I wrote my address and phone number for you on this card." Mary Ann handed him a piece of paper.

"Great, thanks. While I'm thinking of it, here's mine." He handed her a card and shoved her note into his pocket. "What time is your flight tomorrow?"

"I'm flying from Lihue to San Jose at about eleven in the morning."

"My flight is later since I'm going to San Francisco, but how about this? I'll turn my car in early and come to the airport. We can have a last drink before you take off."

"That would be wonderful." Mary Ann felt her heart leap at the thought.

The next morning after packing her bags, Mary Ann picked up her keys and checked the condo to make sure she hadn't left anything. All of a sudden, she realized that she wasn't wearing her dragon lei. She looked through the whole apartment without finding it. In a panic, she dug through her packed suitcase and purse. No sign of it. She couldn't believe she had lost something so valuable, but search as she might, it was gone. She had no choice but to drive her car to the car rental return and take the shuttle to the airport.

Once there, she breezed through security and sat down on one of the padded benches in the central lobby. It was a small airport with only one bar and a small restaurant, two shops and not much more. Time passed, and there was no sign of David. She began to despair of ever seeing him again. She had really believed he wanted to see her once they were back on the mainland. Now it looked like that wasn't going to happen. Certainly she wouldn't call *him*. She could only hope that he might call *her*. Fat chance, she thought. I was just an island fling, someone to spend the evening hours with. Nothing more.

She couldn't help the tears forming in her eyes. Groping in her bag for a tissue, her hand touched a chain of small shells. Her dragon lei! It must have gotten caught in the lining of her bag. She pulled it out with a sigh of relief and fastened it around her neck. At least she would be leaving Hawaii with a remembrance of the wonderful time she had had.

A voice behind her caught her attention.

"I'm so sorry I'm late." David stood there panting slightly. "I got in a little fender bender on the way to the car rental, and by the time I sorted out all the insurance problems, I was afraid I'd missed you. Mary Ann, you know how much you mean to me. I would never leave you."

Mary Ann slid her fingers across the smooth shells around her neck.

"I know," she said smiling up at him.

MIRROR, MIRROR

Norma ran her hand along the row of hangers on the thrift store rack. She needed a new robe. Her old one was wearing out and not warm enough for the cold January mornings. Short of money, she had decided to try the thrift store first. So far, she had found two or three thin rayon wraps as well as a number of faded cotton ones.

Her hand stopped as she felt the heaviness of embroidery on silk. She pulled the hanger out from the rack and couldn't believe what she was seeing. A cream-colored kimono, fully lined and exquisitely decorated with embroidered floral designs on the front. An intricately worked green dragon stretched the length of the back. She took a quick look at the price and rushed to the front of the store with her prize.

At home, she proudly pulled the kimono from its plastic bag and displayed it for her husband Joe to praise.

"Well, it's beautiful all right, but how you gonna' fry bacon in it? Aren't you afraid you'll get it stained?"

"I'll just be extra careful. It was so much nicer than everything else at the store. And it was only five dollars. I couldn't pass it up."

"Okay. But don't come crying to me if you ruin it." With that, he went back to his football game on TV.

The next morning, Norma shivered as her feet hit the cold floor. She grabbed the kimono and pulled it on, slid into her slippers and hurried downstairs to turn on the heat. By the time, her husband came down, the house was warming up and breakfast was cooking.

"I see you're wearing your new robe."

"Yes. I can't believe how warm it is considering it's so light weight."

"Well. So long as you're happy." He settled himself at the table. "Mmm. Those bacon and eggs sure smell good."

As the days went by, Norma continued to be thrilled with her purchase. It kept her warm but didn't feel bulky. She wore an apron when she cooked and as long as she was careful about waving her arms around, she managed to keep it looking fairly pristine.

Passing by the bathroom mirror one day, she noticed that she appeared slimmer than usual. Maybe she was losing weight. At least she hoped so, but the scale registered its same discouraging message when she stepped on it.

Closer examination of her face revealed fewer lines, less bags and lumps. Maybe that new face cream was working. Ever since she had hit fifty, her appearance had gone downhill rapidly. Every once in awhile, she would try some new regimen that was supposed to make her look younger, but until now, nothing had worked.

She turned away from the mirror, sighing over her lost youth. She dragged on an old pair of jeans and a sweatshirt in readiness for her Saturday morning grocery shopping. On the way out, she stopped in front of her husband.

"Joe?"

"Yes?"

"Do you notice anything different about me?"

He looked up from his newspaper. "Nope. Should I?"

"No. I guess not." Disappointed, she shrugged and headed to the store.

That evening, she got undressed, put on the robe and joined her husband in front of the TV. He looked up as she entered the room and did a double take.

"Wow, Norma, you look beautiful."

"That's not what you said this morning."

"Oh, you know me. I just wasn't paying attention. Seriously, what have you been doing to yourself?"

Unwilling to voice her vague suspicion that somehow the kimono was making her look younger and more attractive, she mumbled something about a new face cream. She knew he'd laugh at her if she suggested that the robe had magical powers.

Joe got up and went into the kitchen. He came back with a couple glasses of wine.

"Here's to my beautiful wife." He raised his glass, looking into her eyes in a way he hadn't done for a long time. "I'm a lucky man."

It didn't take long for Norma to realize that she only looked slimmer and younger when she was wearing the kimono. She had gone shopping for new clothes to flatter her new figure. Once in the store, she was devastated to see her reflection in the dressing room mirror. In front of her was the same slightly overweight matronly woman, straining to fit into a garment that was obviously too small. She leaned closer and saw that every line and brown spot on her face was still there. She left without buying anything.

At home, she took to wearing the robe all day and limiting the number of outings she went on. She wondered if she kept wearing it if she would get even younger. She would have to stop wearing it if she began to look like a teenager. She giggled at the thought. Luckily, she seemed to have reached her mid-thirties in appearance and stayed there.

Her husband noticed that she was staying in more and more.

"You're certainly turning into a homebody. Maybe I should take you out for dinner or something. Show you off."

"I like staying home. All those restaurants are too high priced anyway." Norma knew he'd be satisfied with her answer since he really had never liked going out. He was much happier at home with a beer and the television set.

"Still … it seems like you never wear anything but that kimono these days."

"It's comfortable. No sense getting all dressed if I'm not going out. Besides, I like the look. Sort of mysterious and exotic, you know." She gave him a sly look.

"You do look good in it. It's a little long though, sometimes it drags in the back. Maybe you should get it hemmed up."

"No, no. Its fine the way it is. Really." She didn't want to take any chances. For all she knew, altering the length might alter its effect.

As the year wore on, the kimono began to look a little shabby. In spite of all her efforts, spots appeared here and there after she cooked. She washed it by hand not wanting to risk taking it to the cleaners and possibly losing it. The fragile fabric along the bottom began to fray slightly where it occasionally dragged on the floor, and loose threads hung from the edges of the sleeves.

Still Norma continued to wear it every day. She couldn't bear to see what she really looked like, now that she could be her former, younger self as long as she was dressed in the silken robe.

Christmas came and with it, the return of their two children for the holidays. Their daughter, Karen, was in her late twenties and working in a big city some miles away. She didn't get home often since her job was very demanding. She arrived first and gasped when she saw her mother.

"Mom! What have you been doing to yourself? You look like you're thirty. Did you have a facelift?"

"No, no, nothing like that. Just some new facial treatments at the beauty parlor." Norma changed the subject, "I'm so glad you could come for the holidays. It seems like we never see you anymore."

Their son, Steven., now thirty, arrived with his wife, Phoebe, and their two children for an extended stay since they lived even further away.

They all commented on how great she was looking. She smiled and accepted the compliments without revealing her secret. Steven did make an offhand remark about her always wearing the kimono, but she just said she liked being comfortable.

With all the extra mouths to feed, groceries began to run low and Norma announced she'd make a trip to the store the next day. Steven's wife offered to go with her, but Norma said it would be faster if she went alone.

"I know where everything is, and I can just whip through the place to get what we need."

In reality, she didn't want to be seen without the robe on. In spite of what she'd said, it took her over an hour to finish up the shopping and get back home.

Voices from the kitchen could be heard as she came back in the house. She called out, "Bring in the groceries, would you? I'll be down in a minute to put them away."

Then she quickly scooted up to her room to wrap herself in the kimono while they were busy carrying in the bags. She went directly to the hook where it always hung, but it wasn't there. It has to be here, she thought. It was her most valuable possession, and she was very careful to keep it in plain sight. There was no way it could just disappear.

"Surprise!" A chorus of voices sounded behind her.

She turned to see smiling faces on her family members as they crowded into the doorway. Her daughter handed her a big package wrapped in elegant silver paper and adorned with an enormous gold bow.

Norma carefully untied the bow and removed the paper, folding it neatly for future use. She lifted the lid off the box and saw a creamy silk garment richly embroidered with Asian designs.

"We saw how much you loved that old robe you always wear," her daughter said, "but it was getting threadbare, so we bought you a brand new one. It's almost identical, even has dragons on it. We didn't want to wait until Christmas to give it to you. We all chipped in and really hope you like it."

"It's very beautiful, but what happened to the old one?" Norma choked out. She tried to keep the note of desperation out of her voice.

"We know how you save everything. We didn't want you to keep wearing it while you kept the new one for special occasions, so we gave it to the Goodwill. Mom, you don't have to cry." Karen gave her mother a big hug when she saw the tears forming in Norma's eyes. "We wanted to do something really meaningful for you this year, and we're so happy that we found the perfect gift."

PEACE AND QUIET

The words *Imperial Dragons* emblazoned on the back of his black jacket, caught the sunlight as the beefy man swung his leg over his Harley. Three more bikers with the same emblem followed their leader. Scattering gravel, they roared out of the small gas station leaving a cloud of dust in their wake.

"Those darn bikers get more obnoxious every day." Luke, the gas station owner, pushed his hat to the back of his head and ran his fingers through his sparse hair. "The way they tear through here like they owned the place or somethin', making so much noise, you can hardly hear yourself think. Not the peaceful place I had imagined when I was looking to retire."

"I wouldn't want to cross them," his friend, Jim, said. "Did you see the knife scar on that one guy? Not to mention the numbers tattooed on their necks and all the skull and crossbones on their arms. Didn't that one fella have a teardrop under his eye? You know what that means."

"I do. And they're hurting my sales. If it weren't for them, I wouldn't be selling much gasoline at all." Luke sighed. "People in town are leery of coming in now that the bikers are here so often. I think more and more of the locals are filling up on their way home from the city or going up to that new truck stop on the highway. And every time those Dragons come in, I hold my breath. They're looking to cause some trouble, I just know it."

"I've lived here most my life and there's never been a problem. But now …" Jim's voice trailed off.

"Yep. May have made a mistake buying this old place. Wasn't intending to make a huge profit or anything, just somethin' to give me a little spending money over and above Social Security. Seemed like a nice, quiet little town when I first came here."

"It used to be. Don't know why those bikers want to hang out here. There's nothing much to do. Only the one bar and no action to speak of. Seems like they're here every Monday and Friday, now that I think of it."

"So what are they doing here?" Luke asked. "Maybe we should try to find out."

"Are you kidding me? Not a good idea. The further we stay away from them, the better off we'll be."

"I don't know. Wouldn't hurt to just drop by the bar when they're in there. See what we can find out. It's a free country. We're entitled to a beer same as they are – just too old codgers on a night out."

"Well, I guess a beer at the Swing Inn couldn't hurt. When did you want to go?"

"How 'bout Friday night?"

When Friday night rolled around, Jim and Luke strolled into the Swing Inn trying to look like it was just another night out for them.

The bikers had monopolized most of the space along the bar so they took a table in the back and gave a high sign to Maxine, the owner/bartender.

"What can I get you fellas?" Maxine asked.

They both ordered a beer, and she said she would be right back.

After she had plunked down their beers and collected their money, she asked, "What're you guys doing in here on a Friday night? I thought you only indulged at lunch time."

"Oh, just taking a break," Jim said. "Thought we'd check out the local action."

"Local action?" Maxine laughed and waved her arm in the direction of the almost empty room. "Does this look like action to you?"

"What about those guys?" Luke asked, indicating the bikers leaning against the bar. "Though I have to say, they don't look like they're having such a great time. They look bored more than anything."

"Oh, them. They're here every Monday and Friday night. They drink a couple of beers, make a little small talk and leave promptly at ten. They never seem to be enjoying themselves and actually they're pretty much a downer when it comes to business. I've noticed my regulars have stopped coming on those nights."

After Maxine returned to the bar, Luke turned to Jim. "They usually leave at ten. How about we follow them Monday night? See where they go?"

"Oh, right. How are we going to follow them? They'd notice a car right off, and I can't see us with our rummy old legs running down the road after them."

Luke laughed at the mental image. "Say, what about your cousin's old Triumph bike with the sidecar? It's not very loud and we could both ride it. Would he lend it to us?"

"Maybe. I'll ask him."

The following Monday night, Luke and Jim rolled the Triumph into the dark side street by the Swing Inn and waited. At 10 p.m., as Maxine had said, the four bikers pushed their way out of the bar and mounted their Harleys. As they started their engines, the noise easily covered the sound of the old Triumph as it putted into motion.

Jim drove and Luke sat in the sidecar. They stayed well back, but it wasn't really necessary. The bikers seemed to be following a well-worn trail and had no idea anyone would dare follow them. The leader turned left onto a dirt road and the other three followed, leaning into the turn.

"They're heading up to the old Fall Creek Campground," Jim yelled.

"Quiet! They might hear you," Luke warned.

"Doubt it. Couldn't make more noise if they tried," Jim said, but he didn't say anything more.

Eventually, the bikers pulled into the deserted campground and gunned their engines before shutting them down. At the same time, Jim and Luke stopped behind a stand of trees and cut their motor. Quietly they crept towards the open area and hid behind some bushes. The bikers were just standing around, talking in low tones. One dropped a cigarette and ground it into the dirt. Everyone waited.

Jim and Luke had no idea what they were waiting for, but stayed quietly in their places, afraid to even whisper.

After about fifteen minutes, they heard a car approaching the campsite. A dark sedan, it cut its lights and rolled into the open space where the bikers stood. Two men emerged from the car, slamming the doors behind them.

"Let's make this quick," barked the first man out of the car.

"Right," the lead biker answered. "I have the money. Where's the weed?"

"It's in here." One of the men went around to the back of the car and popped the trunk.

Packages were pulled out of the car and handed off to the four men, who shoved them into saddlebags on their bikes. The head Dragon gave an envelope to one of the men from the car and a minute later, all the engines roared to life. The car left first, flicking on its headlights once it was on its way down the road. Shortly after, the bikers headed out.

"What was that?" Luke asked.

"Looked like cash for drugs. Was that the county sheriff or were my eyes deceiving me?"

"Yep," Luke answered. "Sheriff Billy Mason. Law enforcement at its best."

"This is going to be more complicated than we first thought."

"But not impossible for two good old boys like us. Let's get back on home and put our thinking caps on." Luke hiked himself back into the sidecar. Jim started up the engine, and they proceeded slowly back down the mountainside towards town.

The next day, feet propped on the porch railing, Jim and Luke discussed the situation.

"So, every Monday and Friday, the bikers show up, meet Sheriff Mason at the campground and exchange money for drugs. Weed, the one guy said. Where do you think the Sheriff is getting it?" Luke asked.

"Well, there's plenty of land up there to grow marijuana. He and his partner probably harvest as much as they can between visits and have it ready for pickup. They did pack fairly large bundles into their saddle bags. Do that twice a week, you've got a good supply of drugs to sell. A nice bit of cash for everybody involved."

"True. I bet it would be easy to hide the plants under a canopy of trees up there. That campground has been abandoned for a long time. As far as I can tell, no one goes up there at all these days." Luke paused. "There was a story going around about mountain lions in the area, so most folks just avoid the site. Come to think of it, I seem to recall the Sheriff circulated a notice to that effect."

"Uh huh," Jim grunted.

"OK. Here's our problem. We want the bikers to stop coming up here. To do that we have to stop the drug trade. And that means eliminating the source of the drugs as well as the distribution system. We can't notify the county sheriff's office for obvious reasons. So what's our alternative? Could we scare them off?"

"How?" Jim asked. "Bear attacks? Big Foot?"

"No, something more frightening. Real estate developers. How about we spread a rumor that investors are interested in building a resort up there?"

"It might at least slow them down."

"Let's hope."

They immediately began to put their plan into action.

Jim went into the local market and asked the checker if she had heard that a high-priced resort was looking at the campground for possible development. When Luke went to Dave's Barbershop for his haircut, he mentioned that he heard that the campground was being considered for a luxury hotel. It didn't take long for the news to spread through the town.

By the time Friday came around, the whole town was abuzz with the news. Some were all for it. Some adamantly against.

"'Bout time we saw some economic development around here," a realtor said, rubbing his hands together.

"No way. It will ruin the area," one of the older residents remarked. "All those out-of-town rich people roaring through here in their fancy cars. raising prices, looking down on us local folks."

Luke and Jim just smiled and agreed with whichever side they were hearing. The more talk, the better.

Late that afternoon, the bikers again roared into town and hit the bar.

Luke and Jim went up to the campground at nine that night and hid out. When both the bikers and the sheriff's car had arrived, they could hear raised voices. The sheriff was apparently denying any knowledge of the proposed development, the bikers saying they weren't taking any chances.

"This is it. We're calling it quits," the head Imperial Dragon announced. "We're not hanging around until we get caught."

"But it's only a rumor," the sheriff said. "I haven't been able to find out anything definite."

"Doesn't matter. We're too noticeable in this town. People were already talking and now a lot of attention is focused on this campground. We have better sources. As of today, we're history."

One after another the bikers pushed on their starters, raced their engines and roared out of the campground, leaving the sheriff and his companion standing alone in the dark.

About a week later, a fire started in the forest near the campground. Several acres were burned as well as the remains of the old camp buildings.

"Hear about the fire up at Fall Creek?" Luke asked. "Some fool must have dropped a cigarette. The fire crew did a great job of getting it under control quickly."

"Yep," Jim said. "Some of the smoke drifted all the way down here. Smelled a little funny, too. Probably be quite a spell before that part of the forest grows back."

"I hear the plans for a resort have fallen through." Luke leaned back in his chair. "Can't say I'm sorry. I like the town just the way it is. Peaceful and quiet."

ROOM FOR RENT

"Come in."

Hearing the call, Mark hesitantly pushed the door open. He was immediately aware of two blue eyes glaring at him from a brown feline face. Dark ears stuck up like horns in the midst of a ruff of gray fur.

"Um, it's me, Mark," he hollered, afraid to advance any further.

Susan bustled out of one of the backrooms, wiping her hands on a towel.

"Hi. I was expecting you. I can't thank you enough for giving up your day off to help out a fellow slave from the insurance company. Are you prepared to move a lot of furniture?"

"That's what I'm here for, but what is that?" He pointed to the animal seated at eye level on the staircase. The movement caused the cat to narrow her eyes to slits.

"Oh. I forgot to warn you about the Dragon Lady."

"The Dragon Lady?"

"That's what I'm calling her. I got a great deal on the rental of this place, but I had to agree to keep her highness in the style to which she is accustomed.

93

Apparently, she doesn't think lowly humans are here for any other purpose than to serve her. And she is well aware that this is *HER* house."

"But she's a cat."

"Tell her that."

"Right. So what's the deal?"

"I keep her. I feed her. I give her clean water and clean her cat litter every day and in exchange I get a big discount on the rent. Oh, and she is not allowed outside *EVER*. If she should escape this house, I am dead meat. So watch the door at all times, though I have to admit, she hasn't shown any inclination to run for it. She's barely tolerating me and as for anyone else, not at all."

"Is it worth it?"

"Are you kidding me? A great big house, furnished, close to town. And the Dragon Lady hardly ever makes a peep. She looks like she's part Siamese, and they have a tendency to yowl, but she mostly just sits and stares. Hey, I can live with that."

"So, not your average lap cat?"

"I admit I had hoped for a more loving companion, but that doesn't seem to be her nature."

"What happened to her owner?"

"She's in a nursing home."

"Does the cat have a real name?"

"You got me. If she does, no one knows what it is. I think the woman has early Alzheimer's. Isn't too focused, but she wouldn't leave here without knowing the cat was taken care of. Her family just found it easier to agree to her demands than to fight a battle over the animal."

"I see. Well, you got me over here. What do you need moved?" Mark sidled slowly past the cat, not wanting to invite an attack.

"This place is so dark and dingy, I thought I could lighten it up a bit. I've already taken down the heavy drapes and put up some lighter curtains. If we take some of the antiquated furniture pieces and store them in the garage, the rooms will look more inviting."

"Point me in the right direction."

"Okay. Let's start with that really ugly buffet." She indicated an oversized piece of furniture in a corner of what Mark assumed was the dining room. He didn't remember ever living in a house with an actual dining room.

"You have to be kidding. I can't pick that up."

"I know that. I got a dolly and I'll help you."

Together they managed to lift, drag, and push the big sideboard onto the dolly and roll it out to the garage.

When they came back into the house, Mark panted, "How much more?"

"It's harder than I thought," Susan admitted. "Let's just try to move the sofa from hell out of the living room and call it a day."

They went into the living room or what was called the parlor in the day and appraised the offending piece of furniture.

"I guess the Victorians weren't into comfort." Mark pushed down on one of the cushions, but it refused to give.

"To put it mildly. You ought to try sitting on it."

"I'll pass. Let's get this thing out of here. And then I expect a reward."

"Oh, you. Don't get any ideas, but I do have beer in the fridge."

"That will do." Mark proceeded to drag the offending item across the room and, with Susan's help, manhandled it into the garage.

Sweating, Mark plopped down at the kitchen table and took the beer Susan pulled from the refrigerator.

"Thanks. This hits the spot." He took a swallow of the drink. "You know the place already looks better, but why the rush to clear the rooms?"

"The house has four bedrooms and two bathrooms upstairs. I'm going to try and rent out a room. That way the place will almost be free. I'm putting an ad on Craigslist, but I wanted the house to look at least a little inviting before I interview people. Not too many people want to live in a house that looks like the previous owners were the Addams Family."

"Sounds like a plan. I certainly hope your new roommate, whoever he or she might be, appreciates all this effort." Mark set down the now empty can of beer. "I've got to get going. Good luck on finding someone."

"Thanks, Mark. Don't know what I would have done without your help. See you at work on Monday." Susan gave him a kiss on the cheek and closed the door behind him, making sure the cat wasn't lurking by the door in hopes of escape, but there was no sign of the Dragon Lady. The cat seemed to spend most of its time upstairs sleeping. With a sigh of relief, Susan headed to the computer to compose the perfect advertisement in her search for a roommate.

Susan and the Dragon Lady fell into a routine. Every morning before work, Susan put out clean water and food for the cat, inhaled a cup of coffee and headed out to her job as an administrative assistant in a local insurance agency, where Mark was also employed as an agent. In the evenings, the cat greeted her with plaintive meows until the food was put out and then ignored her. On the positive side, the cat seemed to have accepted Susan as her primary person and had started bringing her little gifts from time to time. They were usually chewed-on cat toys, fabric mice or the occasional rabbit's foot. Once, Susan was presented with a real mouse, luckily dead. The pride and the loud meow that accompanied this gift made it obvious that this was a special prize indeed.

"Good cat. Very good cat," Susan assured her while gingerly picking it up with a paper towel and rushing it out to the garbage can.

However, there were days when Dragon Lady disappeared for an hour or two, subsequently appearing with a light decoration of cobwebs on her ears and whiskers. These periods were followed by small pieces of paper scattered in the upstairs hall. At first, Susan just picked them up and tossed them, but then she noticed that they all had writing on them. They appeared to be old letters and, being a nosy person, she began to collect them. However, the fragments were too small to piece together. When she had time, she decided to search out their source.

On Saturdays, she set up meetings with prospective renters at a local Starbucks. The first few interviews didn't go well. She couldn't believe how many losers there were out there. One girl snapped chewing gum incessantly and was between jobs. Another had a laugh that would put a hyena to shame and apparently found everything in the world to be funny. One sniffed and jerked to the point that Susan decided she was on drugs. She began to despair of ever finding an even halfway suitable roommate and began to take the precaution of Googling prospects to eliminate the worst ones before she wasted her time setting up an interview.

Finally on the third Saturday, a well-dressed woman entered the coffee shop and looked around. Having checked her out beforehand, Susan had high hopes. On her Facebook page, she looked normal, employed and friendly. Susan raised her hand and the dark-haired woman headed toward her. Tall and slim, she had striking eyes, slightly slanted up at the corners, dark and penetrating. Similar to the Dragon Lady's, Susan thought.

"Hi. Susan?"

"Yes. Jennifer Walsh?"

"I was hoping I wasn't late," Jennifer said pulling out a chair.

"No. You're right on time." Susan cut to the chase. "You were looking for a room to rent?"

"Yes. The place sounds perfect, actually. It's a nice looking house though older and definitely closer to my work."

"You know the house?"

"Oh, yes."

"How is that possible?"

"Well, when I walked in I recognized you. I drive down that street going and coming from work. Saw you coming out of the house a couple times."

Had she attracted a stalker? Susan thought it was awfully convenient that Jennifer knew where she lived. Still, she seemed normal otherwise.

"Oh." She continued with the interview. "Well, there are four bedrooms upstairs. You could have your choice and your own bathroom. There's a television set in the downstairs living room, but it's pretty old. There's a cable connection so you can have a TV in your room if you want. We can share the kitchen."

"Sounds good. What's the rent?"

Susan named a figure and Jennifer's eyes widened.

"That's really reasonable. What's the catch?"

"The Dragon Lady."

"The who?"

"The Dragon Lady is the resident cat. She comes with the house."

"That's no problem. I like cats. Funny name though."

"Actually, I don't know her original name. The woman who lived there has Alzheimer's, and her relatives weren't close. I just started calling her Dragon Lady because of the way she looks and her demanding ways."

"Well, I'd really be interested in moving in if you'll have me."

"I think it will work out fine." They stood and shook hands. "When can you come?"

"Next week is the first of the month. How about then?"

"That would be great. Here's my phone number if you need to get in touch with me." Susan handed her one of her business cards.

The following week, Jennifer arrived with boxes of clothes and a few possessions including a computer and TV. Susan again pressed Mark into service, and he was there to help carry the boxes up to the room Jennifer had chosen.

Susan had thought it odd that Jennifer picked the smallest bedroom on the floor, but Jennifer had insisted.

"It's just so cozy," she said. "I don't need a lot of space, anyway."

The room she had selected was at the far end of the hall up against what Susan had determined to be some sort of storage area and apparently the Dragon Lady's favorite haunt. Maybe Jennifer just wanted more privacy.

"Now you really owe me," Mark panted as he dragged another box up to the second floor. "What does she have in here, anyway?"

"I have no idea and it's none of your business. How about I cook us all a good dinner to celebrate her first night here?"

"Does a good dinner include wine?"

"If you want it to."

"Then I'm in."

Susan smiled to herself. Men were so easy.

"So what do you think of my new roommate?"

"She seems nice. Maybe a little strange."

"What do you mean? If you wanted strange, you should have seen some of the other applicants."

"I don't know. It's just a feeling I got."

"Oh. Now you're Mr. Psychic."

"No. Forget I said anything. What are we having for dinner?"

"Pasta, okay?"

"Perfect."

When Jennifer came down after unpacking, a big pot of sauce was steaming on the stove and the table was set.

"Wow. This is great." She chose a seat at the table.

"Don't get used to it," Susan said, smiling. "It's a welcome to the house dinner. After this, you're on your own." She dished out the steaming pasta, topping it with sauce and Parmesan. "What would you like to drink?"

"Whatever you're having would be fine."

Susan opened a bottle of merlot and poured them each a glass.

"To our new home." She clinked her glass against the others and they all drank.

Jennifer turned out to be the perfect roommate. She headed up to her room when she got home from work and usually spent the evening there. They each prepared their own dinner or got takeout as the mood struck them. She didn't play loud music, invite strange men home or for that matter entertain anyone. There were occasional loud thumps from her room, but Susan figured she was just exercising or rearranging furniture.

They took turns making coffee in the morning. Then they each grabbed a cup and headed out to their respective jobs. Jennifer worked as a receptionist at a dental office in town. Susan reflected on Jennifer's comment that she happened to be driving by the house before she moved in. The comment was puzzling because the house was way out of the way for someone working at that particular building. However, the issue wasn't important so she didn't ask any questions.

Now that life had settled into a routine, Susan decided to try to find out where the cat was getting all the little papers and ribbons she was playing with. When Jennifer went away with friends for a weekend, Susan started exploring. The upstairs hall ended just past the little bedroom Jennifer had chosen. Susan looked for an entrance to an attic or storage space since she was sure the cat had been bringing things from that part of the house. There was no obvious doorway or trapdoor. She tapped on various parts of the wall and just as she was ready to give up, a panel swung open revealing a small dingy room. The cat squeezed in beside her, weaving in and out of her legs.

A few cardboard boxes were stacked against the wall, but a large trunk with its lid open took up most of the space. One look inside and Susan knew that this was where the cat's treasures had been coming from. Old letters and documents tied with faded and disintegrating ribbon were tossed haphazardly inside. Some had claw marks in them from the cat who obviously thought they made a good scratching pad. The whole conglomeration looked as though a tornado had been through it. Susan picked up one packet of letters and set it aside to look through later.

"Now, Lady, how have you been getting in here?"

The cat gave her a look, lifted a dainty paw and began licking. No answer there.

Susan looked for a way the cat could be getting in and soon found a small narrow space at the top of one of the walls. She pushed and another panel opened. She found herself in Jennifer's room. She noted that the bed had been moved to the other wall. Dust tracks marked the opening of the panel. Had Jennifer wanted this particular room because she knew that there was an entrance to the storeroom? How had she known? Why did she want to go in there?

As Susan thought about it, she realized that since Jennifer had moved in, there hadn't been the usual number of "gifts" strewn along the hall. Apparently the cat's path had been blocked by Jennifer's closed door.

Before she addressed any of these questions, Susan decided to go through the trunk herself. Maybe the answer lay in it. She went back into the storeroom and carefully closed the panel behind her. She grabbed one of the cardboard boxes, dumped out some old clothes and began stuffing the papers into the box. When she had most of them, she topped the pile with the first ribbon-bound letters she had pulled out, dragged the box to her own room and closed the door.

Wiping tears from her eyes, Susan set the last packet of letters to one side. It was an age- old story. Martha White, now old and decrepit, had once been young and beautiful. From the letters, all addressed to her from a Jim Larson, Susan could feel the intensity of their relationship. Martha had become pregnant. Jim had gone to war. In every letter, he pledged his love. He assured her he would return and they would get married. He wanted nothing more than to take care of her and their child. Susan also surmised that Martha had been under considerable censure from her family due to her pregnancy, but had had faith that Jim would come home, and they would be together soon. According to his reassuring responses, it was obvious she had stood up to her family and insisted on having the baby. And then the letters from him stopped.

Martha subsequently married a man named Jonathan Grunewald, and they had two children, the two from whom Susan was now renting. Nothing was ever mentioned about the child she had born as a result of her relationship with Jim Larson. Anything could have happened, but Susan had the feeling that Martha had been forced to put the baby up for adoption. With a sigh, she gathered up the letters and carried them back to the storeroom. It was all just history now and really none of her business. Probably Jennifer had accidentally found the trunk and been equally curious. Or was it something more? Had there been other papers which were now gone? She would probably never know.

A loud meow broke her reverie.

"I know, Lady, it's time for your dinner."

Apparently the cat knew the word "dinner" because she bounded down the stairs with enthusiasm and stood with undisguised impatience when Susan reached the kitchen.

"Really, for a being of your stature, you would think you could find something to eat that didn't smell so bad." Susan wrinkled her nose as she opened a can of cat food, but Lady just dug into the food like it was a gourmet meal. The trunk and its contents were soon forgotten.

As a result, Susan was floored when she entered the kitchen for her morning coffee the next day and Jennifer turned on her with flashing eyes.

"What were you doing in my room?"

"What?"

"My room. Why were you in there?"

"I-I," Susan stammered. "I didn't intend to go in. I was in that little attic at the end of the hall. I was looking for the cat's entrance. I saw this hole at the top of the wall and pushed. The door swung open, and I was in your room. I didn't stay. I just backed out and shut the door. How did you know I'd been there, anyway?"

"I could tell by the track from the door. You stay out of there. Do you hear me? That is my place. You have no right to invade my space."

"Okay, okay, it was an accident." Susan held up her hands and backed out of the kitchen. Wow, she thought. Talk about overreacting.

Heavy rain drummed on the wooden porch, so she grabbed an umbrella and escaped. She was beginning to think Mark had been right. Her roommate was more than a little odd.

It was a long day, and the rain was still coming down in torrents as Susan left work. She was really looking forward to a quiet evening, a hot bath and a glass of wine. But when she turned into her driveway she was appalled to see Lady, drenched to the skin, crying piteously and huddled against the front door.

"Oh, my gosh," Susan cried. "What are you doing out here? You poor thing."

Susan picked the cat up and carried her into the house. She ran for a towel and dried the poor bedraggled animal as best she could.

"Have you been out all day? Did Jennifer let you out? She left after me, but, no, she knows better."

The cat didn't answer but wolfed down the food Susan put out.

A half hour later, the front door banged open, and Jennifer stood in the foyer shaking her umbrella out the door. Susan met her in the living room.

"Jennifer, did you let Lady out this morning?"

"Oh, the cat," Jennifer said. "I didn't *let* her out. She just darted past me and I couldn't catch her."

"She was out all day in that rain."

"So?"

"You should have let me know. I would have come home and let her back in. She was just waiting by the door."

"I didn't think of it. Excuse me, but I'm wet and tired. I'm going up to my room." With that, she ran up the stairs.

Susan didn't know what to believe. The Dragon Lady didn't actually *dart*, stalk was more like it. And in all the time Susan had lived there, she had never shown any inclination to go out the front door. Was leaving her out payback for what Jennifer perceived as an intrusion into her privacy? Ridiculous. With that thought, Susan headed to her well-earned bath. And that would have been the end of it. Except it wasn't.

Over the next few weeks, there was the occasional unusual event. One evening, Susan went into her bathroom and felt there was something wrong. She saw that her cosmetics were arranged as they always had been. Her small collection of pill bottles lined the shelf to the right. Still, there was something out of place. Then she saw it. Her birth control pill container was on the left of the sink instead of the right. She picked it up and looked inside. The pills were arranged by day, and she was one day short. Had she accidentally taken two by mistake one day? She didn't know.

Then there was the missing yogurt. She could have sworn she had bought a dozen containers, but now she was already down to eight, and it had only been two days since she went to the store. Had she miscounted?

She noticed that her best pair of shoes was missing from her closet. How had that happened? She searched everywhere and finally found them under a chair in the living room. For the life of her, she couldn't remember leaving them there.

And Lady was now so happy to see her every evening she was practically clingy. Was Jennifer abusing the cat when Susan wasn't around? There was nothing that she could actually accuse Jennifer of doing, but on the other hand, there were too many little incidents to ignore. It was hard to believe that her perfect roommate could be responsible, but there seemed to be no other explanation.

Susan took a deep breath and prepared for the inevitable unpleasant confrontation. "Jennifer, I need to talk to you," she said.

"What is it?"

"I don't think things are working out here. I'm going to have to ask you to leave."

"What? You're kidding, aren't you?"

"No. Not really."

"What do you mean, 'not working out'?"

"Um. We're just not compatible. It's probably my fault." Susan decided by taking the blame, Jennifer's feelings wouldn't be hurt.

"I thought we had an agreement. Anyway, I'm not leaving."

"What do you mean?"

"I mean, I'm not leaving. Period. This is my place and I'm staying."

"But you can't do that. I'll give you plenty of time to find another place."

"Oh, yes, I can. If anyone is leaving, it's you." Jennifer turned and ran up the stairs.

"Mark, you have to help me."

"What is it, Susan?" he groaned. "More furniture?"

"No. Nothing like that. I think Jennifer is playing little tricks on me. Hiding things, messing with my medications, maybe abusing the cat. I told her she had to leave, and she won't. Now what do I do?"

"That's a problem, all right. Not sure if you can get her out short of calling in the law."

"Oh, my gosh. Really?"

"If she won't leave, what are your options?"

"You're right. It's either law enforcement, move out myself—and I signed a lease so I'm not sure if I can leave, or put up with her. I can't believe this."

"Not good. Why do you think she's doing this?"

"I accidentally went into her room."

"Accidentally? How does that happen?"

"Long story short. I found this storeroom at the end of the hall, and when I pushed on a loose panel, I ended up in her room. I didn't mean to, but it happened. She found out and is blaming me for having entered her 'space'. But here's the kicker. She had been going into the storeroom rummaging through the papers there before I even discovered it."

"Sounds like one of those Nancy Drew 'hidden room' mysteries."

"Well, it sort of is. But I didn't find anything but old love letters. I don't know what she found."

"I hate to say it, but I think you're stuck with her."

"No. Don't say that." Susan buried her face in her hands.

"Try reasoning with her."

"What? Say, please move out. I know the rent is the lowest you can find anywhere, but I don't like you anymore so you have to leave? How is that going to work?"

"I don't know, but that seems to be your best option."

"I'll try." Susan sighed. "If she just stayed to herself I could tolerate her, but messing with my things, picking on the cat. It's bad. Sort of like that movie with Michael Keaton where he wouldn't leave."

"I don't know what else to tell you." Mark gave her a sympathetic look and turned back to his desk.

She went home after work and steeled herself for a conversation with Jennifer, but Jennifer never showed. Susan finally dragged herself to bed, exhausted from the tension and anticipated argument. Lady must have felt the same way because, for the first time, she jumped onto Susan's bed and went to sleep cuddled against her legs.

The next few days, there was no sign of Jennifer. Susan began to hope that she was actually leaving. But then things came to head. When Susan entered the kitchen, Jennifer was standing there. "You have to leave."

Susan was astounded. That was her line.

"What?"

"This is rightfully my house, and I can prove it. I don't want you here."

"But I have a lease with the owners."

"Ha! Owners. I'm the owner. Those two are just hangers-on."

"What do you mean?"

"My grandmother was Martha White, and now I can prove it. I got the birth certificate and adoption papers from the trunk. I've seen a lawyer. In a short time, I'll not only own part of this house but have a large share in the inheritance."

"So you only moved in here to get access to the attic?"

"Yes, my mother researched her birth records before she died. The house was on the market at the time, so I stopped by here one day. Told the old lady that I was looking to buy. Doddering old fool showed me all around the place, even pointed out the secret storeroom. I hoped there would be something in there that would help me get the money, and there was."

"So, it's all about money?"

"What isn't?"

"Well, until I see some legal papers, I'm staying," Susan said.

"Oh, really. We'll see about that."

Jennifer turned and stomped out of the room.

Things got worse. Now that there was no attempt at hiding her intentions, Jennifer went into an all out assault. Breaking makeup bottles on the floor of the bathroom, throwing food that had just been purchased into the trash, even slashing some of Susan's clothes. As for the cat, the poor thing now huddled against Susan every chance she got, all arrogance put aside.

Susan had to face the facts. The woman was insane, and things would only get worse. She told Mark her troubles, and he said he would help her find another place to live. She also notified the owners since her lease was still in effect. They were sorry to see her go, but were aware of the lawsuit Jennifer had filed. They released her from the rental agreement, and she was able to move into a small apartment near work. As she was packing to leave, the cat looked at her with what she took as desperation.

"I'm sorry, Lady. There's nothing I can do."

Susan looked back at the animal as she left. She had a bad feeling about leaving her with Jennifer since she had begun to wonder who the real Dragon Lady was, the cat or Jennifer?

A couple of weeks went by and Susan settled into her new apartment. She missed the roominess and convenience of the house. She even sort of missed the cat, but she definitely didn't miss the crazy roommate. She wondered how Jennifer was doing.

It wasn't long before she found out.

Mark accosted her as she came into the office. "Did you hear about Jennifer?"

"No. What?"

"She's dead."

"Come on. Are you kidding me?"

"No, really. I read it in the paper today. Look." Mark pointed at an article on the front page.

Susan picked up the paper and read.

LOCAL WOMAN FOUND DEAD IN HOME

The story went on to say that it appeared that Jennifer Walsh, currently the only occupant of the house, had been found dead by a fellow employee, who had been sent to the home to check on her. She had not been answering her phone, and it was unusual for her to be absent from work without notifying the office. The death appeared to be an accident. It seemed she had slipped on a cat toy and fallen down the stairs. A mouse made of rabbit fur was found halfway down the steps. The neighbors confirmed that the old woman who owned the house had left her cat in the care of the renter.

Susan gasped. Had the Dragon Lady somehow gotten revenge on Jennifer for mistreating her? There had been no love lost between them, and Susan had wondered if Jennifer was abusing the cat. Still, it had to have been an accident like the police said. Ridiculous to even think the cat might have deliberately left her toys where Jennifer could trip on them. Although she didn't remember Lady playing with a mouse like that while she lived there. In fact, now that Susan thought about it, the cat had never been much interested in toys and had seldom even bothered to move them around except for the few she had brought Susan as gifts.

Now that the house was empty again, the owners contacted Susan and asked if she would like to move back in. She jumped at the chance, and the next weekend she opened the front door to see a pair of blue eyes staring at her.

"Hi, Lady. I brought you a treat." She held out the piece of shrimp she had picked up on the way. She didn't think the cat could have had anything to do with Jennifer's death, but …better safe than sorry.

SEEING STARS

Melanie sighed as she trudged into her 8 a.m. astronomy class. *Talk about boring.* When she signed up for the class, it had seemed more interesting than some of the other sciences. She needed two to graduate, and she had already waded her way through geology.

As it turned out, the astronomy professor never spoke above a monotone, there was math involved and she had to struggle to stay awake given the early hour.

She felt her head jerk as she nodded off for the third time and came fully awake on hearing him raise his voice.

"So, I'll see you all this evening at the observatory located on the lower campus. Do you all know where it is?"

There were a few confused looks, but most of the class nodded.

"Good. Attendance is mandatory in order to pass this class. The skies are supposed to be clear so we should be able to view the constellations we've been discussing. Class dismissed."

She gathered up her books and started for the door. *Great, now she had to spend the evening in class as well.*

"Wait up," a male voice called from behind her.

She looked around and didn't see anyone else near her. Turning, she saw a tall, rather skinny classmate hurrying towards her. He wasn't bad looking behind dark rimmed glasses, his blond hair falling across one side of his forehead. He was wearing a blue and gold jacket with the University insignia and faded jeans.

"Who me?" she asked.

"Yes, uh, I was wondering if you would like me to walk with you to the observatory tonight. It's dark on campus, and it would probably be safer if we went together."

"That's awfully nice of you. I am a little nervous about walking alone since it's in a remote part of the campus. I live in the dorms."

"I can swing by there on my way from the frat house. I'm Doug Ely by the way."

"Melanie Scott."

"Okay, Melanie. What say I meet you at the front door of the dorm at twenty of eight?"

"That would be great. Thanks."

"See you then," he said and jogged off, back pack over one shoulder, obviously in a hurry to get to his next class.

That was interesting, she thought to herself. *I wonder if he's going to ask me out.*

She didn't get many dates, not that she was horrible looking or anything. She was short, only five foot four, small boned, with rather messy dark brown hair. Add in the fact that she was forced to wear eyeglasses to see where she was going. Most guys passed her by without a second glance. On the plus side, she had large brown eyes, regular features and a trim figure.

That evening, she shivered as she stood in front of the dorm's main door. *He's probably not going to show up,* but just as she had the thought, she saw him hurrying towards her on the path that led from the fraternity houses.

"I'm not late, am I?" he asked as he approached.

"No. Right on time."

"Good, let's get going then."

Melanie had to scurry to keep up with his long stride. "So, what made you pick astronomy as a science?" she asked.

"Well, I'm really interested in space exploration. Hope to work at NASA some day so this looked like a good place to start."

"Wow. That's great. I'm having a terrible time focusing in class. The professor is a little boring, don't you think?"

"He does leave something to be desired in the presentation department," Doug laughed. "But the subject is really interesting."

"What exactly are we looking at tonight? I think I missed what he said."

"Constellations."

"Oh, right."

"Here we are." Doug pointed at the small campus observatory.

Once inside, they signed the attendance sheet and milled around with the other students until the professor called them to attention.

"Tonight we are going to be observing several constellations," he said, "among them the Big and Little Dippers and the Draco or dragon constellation. It's circumpolar, which means it revolves around the north pole and can be seen all year in our hemisphere. To identify it, note the four stars that form a trapezoid above the Big Dipper. That is its head, the body and tail trail down between the Big Dipper and Little Dipper. It was one of forty-eight constellations listed by Ptolemy in the second century and is one of the eighty-eight known today. It is notable for encompassing several galaxies. You will each have a turn at the telescope after which you may leave."

The students formed a line, each looking into the view finder and turning away. When both Melanie and Doug had had their turn, they started back towards the dorm.

"Well, did you see a dragon?" Melanie asked.

"Sort of, I guess."

"All I saw was a bunch of stars."

Doug laughed. "OK, you got me. That's what I saw, too. Those ancient civilizations had really great imaginations!"

They strolled across the campus, moon and stars providing atmosphere. Doug quietly took her hand as they approached the dorm door.

"So, I'll see you in class next week?" he asked.

"Absolutely. Thanks so much for going to the observatory with me."

"No biggie. See you next week."

With that, Doug turned away and left Melanie standing at the door.

She climbed the stairs to her room, wondering why he hadn't asked her out.

"Well, what happened?" her roommate, Liz, asked as soon as she came into the room. Melanie had told her about Doug while she was getting ready to go out.

"Nothing, actually. He just said he'd see me next week in class. Darn, he's really a nice guy."

"Bummer. Maybe he's shy. I'd try pushing it a little at class next week. Maybe say you need help with your homework. Could he do coffee? Something like that."

"That's all I can do, I guess." Melanie flopped down on her bed and stared at the ceiling.

The following week, Melanie couldn't wait to get to class. She scanned the room as she entered, but saw no sign of Doug. The clock ticked towards the hour, and the professor took up his place in front of the class. An hour later, Doug had still not appeared. As the students rose from their seats, she made her way over to the blonde that usually sat next to Doug.

"Hi. You know the guy that sits here?" She pointed to the empty seat.

"You mean the nerd? Don't really know him. He doesn't talk much, just 'Hi' and that's pretty much it."

"So you don't know what fraternity he belongs to?"

"Sorry, I don't." She gathered up her books. "You interested in him?"

"Oh, no. I just borrowed some class notes from him. Wanted to return them. He'll probably be here next week. Thanks."

Melanie headed to the student union building hoping she might see him though she had never noticed him there before. No sign of him, but she spied her roommate sipping a latte at one of the tables. She pulled out a chair and slumped down in it.

"What happened? Did he shine you off?"

"No. He didn't show at all, which is odd because he's really into learning as much as he can about space and all."

"Maybe he's sick. He'll probably be there next week."

"Great. By that time, he'll have forgotten all about me."

"So remind him. I gotta run. My next class starts in ten minutes. Catch you later."

The week dragged on, but then on Friday night something happened that made Melanie even more anxious to find Doug. She was walking home from the library after dark when a large hand grabbed her arm, pulling her off the path.

"Tell me where he is," a gruff voice said into her ear.

"Who?"

"You know. Your boyfriend."

"I-I don't have a boyfriend."

"Who do you think you're kidding? We saw him with you."

"What do you want? Please don't hurt me."

"Oh, we'll hurt you all right. You tell him he'd better produce or he's going to be out one cute little girlfriend."

"I'm telling you. I don't know who you're talking about."

"I know you're lying. You tell him."

As suddenly as he'd grabbed her, the man pushed her down on the ground and strode away. He was joined by another man, also very big. From the back they looked like linebackers or at least what she thought linebackers looked like.

Melanie ran stumbling towards the dorm, tears streaming down her face.

Liz looked up as she entered the room and gasped.

"What happened to you?"

"Some guys attacked me on the way home from the library."

"Oh, no, did they…?"

"No, nothing like that. They just kept asking about my boyfriend. I told them I didn't have one, but they didn't believe me."

"Do you think they meant Doug?"

"They said they had seen me with him, and he's the only guy I've even been near lately. Maybe they did mean him. They said to tell him to 'produce' or they would do something awful to me. What am I going to do? I'm scared. Do you think I should report it to the campus police?"

"The guys didn't hurt you, did they? And what could the police do? It's not as if you know who they are. I think I wouldn't go through the hassle. Maybe it was a case of mistaken identity. You'll probably never see them again."

"I hope you're right. But, anyway, I can't wait until class next week. I have to talk to Doug."

Relief made Melanie's body sag as she entered the classroom and saw Doug sitting at his usual place. Hoping to talk to him before class, she made her way to his seat, leaned over and said into his ear, "I have to talk to you, now."

At that moment, the professor cleared his throat and told them to take their seats. There was nothing to do but wait. Melanie went back to her chair and for once, she didn't fall asleep. As soon as the class ended she made a beeline for the door to make sure Doug didn't decide to leave without her.

She needn't have worried though. He came right to her and for the first time she saw the other side of his face. It was covered with black and blue bruises, and there was a big cut across one cheek.

"What happened to you?" she gasped.

"Oh. Took a wrong step on the cement steps up to our house. Landed on my face as you can see."

"Right. Did they do that to you?"

"What do you mean 'they'? What did you want to talk about?"

"The other night, two men grabbed me as I was walking back from the library. They threatened to hurt me if I didn't get 'my boyfriend' to 'produce'. I think they meant you since you were the only guy I could have been seen with recently, not that I like to admit it."

Doug rubbed his face and winced at the pain. "Now I've dragged you into this."

"Dragged me into what?"

"It's sort of complicated. A month or so ago, I had a financial crisis. Not enough money for rent, books. You know how it is. Anyway, I noticed that this big guy sitting next to me in English 101 was really struggling. He's on a football scholarship and has to keep his grades up. I didn't tell him, but I have an eidetic memory. I can visualize anything that I've read so exams and papers are easy for me." Doug shrugged and continued, "I offered to help him with the class if he would pay me. He jumped at the opportunity, but as the days went by, I ended up doing all his work for him. I made errors and kept the level of skill low so it would look like he was doing the work. When some of his athlete buddies found out, they insisted I help them, too. I did at first, but was really nervous since I even had to sit in some classes and take tests as if I were them. Finally, I just refused to help them anymore. I'm afraid of getting caught, maybe getting expelled, and there would go my future in NASA. They're trying to force me into taking their finals, witness the results of my recent 'accident'. I've been avoiding them as best I can. But now, they're threatening you, and I'm up against it."

"Well, there must be something we can do," Melanie said. "We need to think about it. Why don't we meet this evening and put our heads together?"

"All right. I have a late class. How about seven at the Student Union?"

"OK. See you there," Melanie said and hurried off to her next class. *How did I get mixed up in this? One semi-date with a cute guy and look what happened.*

That evening, the two of them sat, drank coffee and tried to brainstorm their way out of the mess they were in. Tired and at a loss, they started walking back to the dorms, still throwing out possible solutions that didn't involve transferring to another school or dropping out for the rest of the semester.

The next thing they knew they were surrounded by four large men. One grabbed Melanie, and Doug charged him. One of the other men had a large stick and swung it at Doug, hitting him in the head. Doug fell like a rock.

"Stupid," the one holding Melanie yelled. "You hit him too hard. Let's get out of here."

"We'll be back," the last man called over his shoulder as he ran. "We're not done with this."

Melanie tried to revive Doug, but he was truly out and blood was streaming from his head wound. She pulled out her phone and called for an ambulance.

When the EMT's arrived, they loaded Doug into the back of the vehicle.

"How did this happen?" one asked.

"We were joking around, and he hit his head on a low tree branch," Melanie lied.

"Okay. We're taking him to the University Med Center."

They drove off. Melanie wanted to follow, but it was on the lower campus, a long dark walk so she returned to the dorm. Despite several calls to the hospital that night, she was unable to find out how he was doing.

The next morning she hiked down to the Med Center and, once there, she was told that Doug was out of danger and resting comfortably.

"Can I see him?"

The nurse checked his chart and said the doctor had approved visitors. Doug appeared to have normal responses and would probably be released the next day. They would want him to come back for some tests since there was some brain trauma, and it would be awhile before they would know if the injury had caused him any permanent damage.

Melanie stuck her head in his door. "Hi. Are you up to seeing people?"

"You're not 'people', come on in. I'm glad to see you're all right, I was worried. They didn't hurt you, did they?"

"No, they ran off when they saw they had knocked you out."

"What did you tell the ambulance guys?"

"I said we were fooling around, and you hit your head on a low branch."

"Good. We don't want anyone to know what's really going on."

"Well, at least you're safe here in the hospital. And I think they will back off for a little while. They don't want word getting around either."

"Right." Doug's eyelids started to droop.

"You're tired. I'll come back tomorrow and make sure you get home safely," Melanie said. "Oh, by the way, I seem to have lost some of my astronomy notes. What was the name of that dragon constellation we saw the other night? Drago? Draco?"

Doug rubbed his head, and with a sheepish grin said, "I can't remember."

TOO MUCH OF A GOOD THING

Jane loved walking near the pond behind her house. It was a peaceful place, calm and yet teeming with life. The tranquil surface of the water, here and there covered with spots of light green algae, reflected the surrounding marsh plants. The blade-shaped leaves of the butterfly iris with its ethereal blooms, so fragile and short-lived, lent an air of magic to the place.

As she wound her way along the path, she spied a stunning dragonfly, bright red against the varying shades of green that bordered the water. Fascinated, she watched as it balanced on the very tip of a spiky leaf, unmoving, a part of the landscape but too colorful to be overlooked.

The sun beat down on her back, and there wasn't the faintest hint of a cooling breeze. A bead of sweat trickled down the side of her face. Sighing, she turned and walked back up to the house and the cooling presence of the air conditioner.

"I saw the most beautiful dragonfly down by the pond," she told her husband, Bob, when she entered the kitchen. As usual he had his nose in the newspaper and a cup of coffee clutched in his hand. "I wish I'd had my camera with me so I could have gotten a picture."

Bob looked up from his paper. "Where there's one dragonfly, there are bound to be more. I read somewhere that they only grow wings when they are about to mate." Spouting little known facts from his encyclopedic memory was one of his more annoying habits, but could come in handy on occasion. In fact, Jane kept suggesting he try to get on "Jeopardy", but he just mumbled something about not making a fool of himself on national TV.

"Why don't you take your camera down tomorrow morning and see if any show up?" he added.

An amateur photographer, Jane loved to get close-up photos of nature and was struggling to put together a portfolio that she wouldn't be embarrassed to show to the local art gallery. She was exceptionally critical of her own work, and more prints ended up in the trash than in the leather portfolio given to her by her children. Now that they were grown and living several hours away, she was free to pursue her art. What's more, they recognized her talent and thoroughly approved of healthy outdoors activities for their retired parents. Bob had golf. Jane had photography.

Early the next morning, Jane picked up her camera and headed out to the pond. It wasn't long before a bright red dragonfly buzzed by her. When it landed on the tip of a leaf, Jane focused her camera and took several shots from different angles.

"You know what would be great?" she said to the dragonfly. "If you could get a few of your friends to come here, too. A picture of one dragonfly is good, but more than one in the shot would be even more impressive."

Good grief, she thought to herself, *I'm talking to a bug. Maybe the kids are right, I need to get out more.*

Smiling to herself, she packed up her camera and headed back to the house.

"I'll be back tomorrow," she called to the dragonfly as she strolled away. "Just in case you do bring some friends."

The next day, much to her delight, there were indeed several more red dragonflies perched atop the leaves. She snapped a number of pictures and happily went back to her studio to develop them. She spent the rest of the day culling the less impressive shots and studying the rest to decide which ones to include in her permanent collection.

At breakfast the following morning, Bob asked, "Have you looked outside today?"

"No, why?"

"Just look."

Jane took her cup of tea to the kitchen window that looked out over the backyard and the field beyond. The pond was now dotted with patches of red.

"Oh, my gosh. How many are there?"

"A lot," Bob answered, squinting. "It looks like hundreds, but it's hard to tell from here. Are you going to go down and take more pictures?"

"Absolutely," she said and, without stopping to dress, she shoved her feet into her gardening shoes and grabbed her camera. Her blood racing, she rushed down the hill, slowing as she approached the pond for fear of startling the little creatures. She didn't want to cause a mass exodus before she could get a picture. But she needn't have worried. They all sat quietly on their perches, wings fluttering slightly. Almost as if they were posing for their photo.

It was an incredible sight. A light breeze riffled the foliage, and she happily clicked away as the little red insects bobbed atop the swaying leaves.

Back in the house, she found Bob sitting in his usual place at the table.

"I Googled dragonflies while you were down there," he announced. "They do sometimes swarm. That's probably what happened here."

"Whatever the reason, I'm thrilled. I've gotten some amazing pictures." She rushed past him, camera in hand. "I can't wait to print them and see how they turned out."

As she brought them up on the computer, she had trouble selecting the ones she wanted to keep. They were all amazing, some of her best pictures so far. If she could keep up this quality of work, she knew she would be able to impress one of the gallery owners, possibly even get a show of her own.

The rest of the day passed quietly, and the next morning Jane backed the car out of the garage on her way to do the weekly grocery shopping. Bob had already left for his golf game. Once in the driveway, she saw that there were little red bodies spaced evenly along the barbed wire fence that separated their property from her neighbor's pasture. It was amazing the way each one perched on top of a vertical spike of wire. As she gazed at them, she suddenly imagined all those multi-faceted eyes staring at her. It actually was a little creepy, she thought with a shake of her head.

At the grocery store, she asked the checker if he had heard any stories about an excessive number of dragonflies in the area.

"Nope, nobody's said nothin' about dragonflies," he answered. "You havin' a problem?"

"Not a problem, exactly. There just seem to be a lot of them out where I live."

"Well, everybody knows they don't bother people. Eat mosquitoes, I hear."

"Then we should be mosquito free this year." She gave a nervous little laugh.

She ran a few more errands and on her return, she thought that maybe there were more of them along the fence than when she had left, but then, who was counting? She put the little insects out of her mind and unpacked the groceries. If it hadn't been so hot out, she would have relaxed on the patio, but the heat was still oppressive so she picked up a book, sank into an easy chair and promptly fell asleep. When she awoke, it was dusk. Bob would be home soon so she hurried about the kitchen, fixing a late dinner just as he pulled into the garage. Then they watched a little TV and called it a night.

"Jane. Jane! Wake up!" Bob's voice was much louder than usual as he called to her from the kitchen.

"What? What is it?" Groggy with sleep, she stumbled down the stairs unhappy at having been so rudely awakened.

"Look outside." His face was flushed, and he was pointing toward the window.

Jane gasped as she peered through the glass. As far as she could see, there was a sea of undulating red. She ran to the front of the house. There, too, the yard was covered with a flickering red mass. She tried to see past the dragonflies, but it seemed there was no end in sight.

She covered her face with her hands. "What are we going to do?"

"We know they won't hurt us," Bob said, "but, I don't know about you, I'm not too anxious to go out there."

"We *know* they won't hurt us. How do we know?" Her voice had risen to a screech.

"According to the internet, they won't. Well, there was this one story about them sewing people's eyes shut, but that's just an old wives' tale."

"That sounds like a myth for sure. But still there's so many of them. How are we going to get out of the house? They could overwhelm us. Imagine them all landing on us, covering our bodies like they did the yard." She brushed her arms at the thought. "The first one was pretty. But hundreds, maybe thousands? Should we call the police? Or an exterminator? Animal control?"

"I think this falls outside of their areas of expertise."

"We could call the kids," she suggested.

"And tell them what? We want you to take the day off and drive over here because we're surrounded by dragonflies. They'd show up all right, and they'd bring the proverbial little men in white coats with them."

"You're right. We're adults. We should be able to handle this ourselves. Besides I'd hate to think of them having to battle their way through all those insects to get to us. And what good would it do? We'd still have to wade through them to escape. What if we fell? What if they smothered us?"

"On the positive side," Bob said, "I also read that they only live about three weeks after they get wings." He paused, reached for her hand and said, "I hope you stocked in a lot of food."

A New Wrinkle

"Hey, look at this article." Megan waved a tabloid at her friend, Amy.

"Mmmhmm." Amy sipped the last of her soda.

"No, really, look. It says here Lady Gaga uses dragon's blood as a liquid facelift."

"Megan, you shouldn't believe everything you read. Especially in those papers you pick up at the grocery counter. I mean, alien babies? Little men from outer space? And now dragon's blood? Who do you think is finding and killing these so-called dragons for their blood?"

"Okay, okay. I get the point. Oh, wait, it turns out that the blood isn't from real dragons."

"What a relief. I wouldn't want cruelty to dragons on my conscience."

"Very funny. No, actually it's red sap from a dragon blood tree. Fairly rare, I guess."

"In that case, it must cost a mint. Come on, we're going to be late getting back to work." Amy rose, picked up her tray and headed to the trash can next to the door.

Megan folded the newspaper and shoved it in her bag as she got up from the table. Maybe it wasn't terribly expensive. She certainly could use a little help in the skin department. She had actually found a couple wrinkles at the corners of her eyes. Well, admittedly, she had to scrunch up her eyes to see them, but it was a sign of things to come.

The two women, friends since their high school days, both worked as clerks for the Dodd, Johnson & Lucas law firm in downtown Sacramento. There had been several openings for low level data entry positions when they graduated, and they applied for the positions in hopes of working somewhere together. When they were hired, they thought it would be a great place to meet men. Eligible lawyers, all looking like Matthew McConaughey, roaming the halls. And the added perk of having inside knowledge about exciting court cases like those portrayed on the legal thrillers they both watched on television.

In reality, it was dull and routine and most of the lawyers were old, married or totally unattractive. Now in their twenties, Amy and Megan were beginning to worry that they'd never find boyfriends. Amy, an attractive brunette on the thin side, was the more down to earth of the two. Megan, a slightly plump blonde, was in the habit of pursuing a new interest on a weekly basis. Over the years, Amy learned to ignore these sudden enthusiasms, aware that they faded as fast as they flowered.

Back at her desk, Megan powered up her computer and concentrated on the deposition she was entering into the database, the newspaper story forgotten. However, later in the day during a lull in her work schedule, she pulled up the internet and began a search for dragon's blood.

That evening as they shared dinner in Amy's apartment, Megan brought up the subject again.

"So, Amy, you know that dragon's blood stuff I read about today?"

"Yes." Amy gave a long suffering sigh.

"Well, I had time to search the net, and I found it."

"That's great, Megan. What should we have for dinner? I can make spaghetti or there's left over Chinese food from the other night."

"I say Chinese."

"Ok." Amy pulled takeout containers from the refrigerator and set the orange chicken, rice and chow mein on the counter. Opening a bottle of Merlot, she poured them each a glass and plopped down in a chair next to the kitchen table. "Warm up whatever you'd like."

"Will do." Megan picked up her glass and sipped her wine, then went back to the subject at hand. "So, guess how much it costs."

"A hundred dollars? Two hundred?"

"Well, more than that, I guess. There were a lot of sites offering dragon's blood, different lotions and prices. I didn't pick a specific one. The trees apparently grow on some island off of Africa and, according to the internet, they're endangered. So now people are planting them other places to make sure they don't die out. But most of them are on that island. Anyway, I thought I'd order some."

"Are you crazy? We barely make enough to go out on Saturday nights."

"But if it would make my skin younger—"

"I hate to point out the obvious, but you're twenty-five. Your skin *is* young."

"I'm not getting any younger, there is no man in my life, and I thought maybe I could prevent wrinkles with it. Be proactive, you know?"

"Fine. But don't come crying to me if you spend all that money, and it doesn't do anything."

"Lady Gaga…"

"Stop, already. She just looks good 'cause she's covered up with lots of makeup and weird hairdos."

Megan got up and started poking through the Chinese food. She spooned a sampling from the containers onto a plate and slid it into the microwave.

"Smells good." She pulled out the plate and picked up a pair of chopsticks.

"Just think about it, okay?" Amy repeated. "Before you blow your next paycheck on an unnecessary face cream. Now, what should we watch tonight? I think "American Idol" is on." She picked up the remote and started scanning the listings.

Megan swallowed the last of her food and stood up, carrying her dish over to the sink.

"I think I'll head home. Get out of these clothes. Thanks for the dinner. See you tomorrow."

"Right. See you at work." Amy clicked on a channel.

The following week Megan rushed home every day after work instead of dropping by Amy's. Not even a free meal got her interest.

"You're not fooling me, you know," Amy said at lunch a few days later. "You ordered that stupid cream and can't wait for it to come in the mail. That's why you're in such a hurry to get home."

"True," Megan admitted, "but you'll be jealous when you see what a difference it makes. Wait and see."

Several weeks later, as the two women were consuming their usual burger and fries, Megan said, "Well?"

"Well, what?"

"Well, can't you see the difference in my skin? It's way smoother."

Amy squinted but couldn't see any change. Still, she didn't want to hurt her friend's feelings.

"Wow, yes, it does look better," she lied.

"I knew it. I've almost finished the first jar so I ordered another one."

"Whoa, can you afford that? I mean it's only been a couple weeks. That's a big expenditure in one month."

Megan looked sheepish. "I charged it."

"Megan, don't be running up your credit cards for that stuff. You can get in a lot of trouble that way. You know you can't live the lifestyle of the rich and famous unless you *are* rich and famous."

"I'll figure something out."

In the weeks that followed, Amy saw less and less of Megan. She would invite her over for dinner, but Megan always declined, saying she was tired and was just going to head home. And, Amy had to admit, she did look tired.

On Saturday nights, they were in the habit of hitting a couple bars in mid-town, sharing a few laughs and occasionally meeting a guy, though none of them ever turned out to be "keepers." Now Megan wasn't interested, and Amy had to go alone or with some of the other single women she knew. She missed the fun the two of them used to have and decided to find out what was really going on.

Winter was coming on, and the evenings were dark by six thirty, so Amy pulled her car up a few doors away from Megan's apartment and waited to see if she would come out. At seven, Megan came clacking through the front door wearing extra high heels, a dark coat wrapped around her. She got in her car, which was parked further up the block. When she pulled out, Amy followed. According to the guidelines from the crime novels she read, she knew to keep a few cars in between them. It wasn't hard to spot Megan's bright red bug in the traffic ahead.

They headed south on Howe Avenue, and, once over the American River, they traveled further and further into some of the poorer neighborhoods of south Sac. Megan pulled into a parking lot behind a shabby looking bar and got out, still clutching her coat around her although it wasn't that cold this particular evening. She went in the back door of the bar, and Amy parked her car nearby.

Now Amy was really worried. Could Megan be stripping or pole dancing? Surely she couldn't be that hard up for money. Amy wasn't all that anxious to go in, given the disreputable appearance of the place, but she had to know. She sidled in through the front door and looked around. It was very dark, and a light haze of cigarette smoke lingered in the room. Obviously the no smoking law wasn't very stringently enforced. There were a number of rowdy drunks seated at the bar yelling at a game displayed on several large TV's. No stage or pole in sight, she thought thankfully. A huge groan went up from the spectators as a receiver dropped a pass. Just then Megan, dressed in a skimpy costume and carrying several drinks on a tray, began weaving her way between tables. Before Megan could catch sight of her, Amy ducked back outside, got in her car and drove home.

At lunch the next day, Amy decided to clear the air.

"So Megan," she began, once they had picked up their food and seated themselves in a booth. "What is it you've been doing that keeps you so busy? I miss having you around."

Megan blushed, "I've been seeing someone."

"Oh? What's he like? Why haven't I met him? He's not married, is he?"

"No, no, no. Nothing like that."

"Did you meet him at that bar you're working in?"

Megan gasped. "How did you know?"

"I followed you."

"You followed me? Why would you do that?"

"Because I was worried about you. And, apparently, with good reason. Why are you working there?"

"I ran up my credit cards and couldn't even make the minimum payments. Mean people started calling me demanding money. So I borrowed money from one of those cheap cash places to pay the charges, and then the interest was so high, I couldn't pay them. Now they're threatening me."

"So, there is no boyfriend."

"No. I just thought that would be a good excuse for not going out with you."

"How much do you owe?"

"I can't bare to say it aloud." Megan pulled a piece of paper towards her and wrote down a figure.

"That much?"

"Mmmhmm and I still don't make enough money to pay off the loan in spite of working the extra job. Oh, Amy, what am I going to do?" A tear slid down Megan's cheek.

"I think it's time for you to see a lawyer."

"I don't know any lawyers."

"Megan, where do we work, for gosh sakes? Just talk to one of them."

"I meant no lawyers in other firms. I can't just go up to my supervisor, Mr. Lucas, and tell him I've been an idiot."

"That's exactly what you should do."

"No! You can't mean it."

"Yes, I do. After you get over the initial fear of approaching him, you'll feel a lot better. And I'm sure he can come up with a solution."

"I can't, Amy. It's too embarrassing. And I can't ask my parents. They're barely making it on Social Security.

What about you? Even a small loan would help me get on top of this thing."

"You know I'd lend it to you, but I just don't have that kind of money. It's Lucas or nothing, I'm afraid."

"What if he fires me? I'll be in worse shape than I am now."

"Those quick cash places are pretty ruthless. They'll probably garnish your wages, and then the law firm will know anyway. You're a good employee, and he seems to be a fair man. I think you have to take the chance."

"What choice do I have? I guess I'll have to suck it up and hope for the best." Megan pushed her food away. "I seem to have lost my appetite."

The next morning, Megan dressed in her best clothes, walked into the office and, taking a deep breath, requested an appointment with the youngest of the law partners. A half hour later, Lucas's private secretary came up to Megan, who was waiting in his outer office.

"Mr. Lucas will see you now," she announced, holding the door open.

Megan stood, smoothed her skirt and walked through the doorway. She had only been in his office when she was interviewed for the job, and then she had been too nervous to take in her surroundings. Now she noticed how intimidating the room was. Bookshelves lined the walls, each stocked with hundreds of thick books. A large desk and several chairs all in some kind of dark wood crowded the available floor space. Feeling small and overwhelmed by the impressive surroundings, she sat down on the edge of the chair facing the desk and tapped her fingers nervously on the arm.

Lucas, a kindly, slightly balding man, looked up from the papers on his desk and fixed a penetrating gaze on her.

"How can I help you, Megan?"

Blinking back tears, she stared down at her hands and stuttered out her story, ending with the trouble she was now in. He listened quietly, steepled his fingers together on the desk and frowned.

"Well, you have certainly gotten yourself in a fix, but I think we can remedy the situation. I'll make a few calls to get the loan sharks off your back, and then we can work out a loan from the firm, which you can pay back in installments. As long as you don't start charging on your cards again, you should be free and clear in a year or so. Of course, you will have to tighten your belt a bit to make ends meet. Oh, and quit that waitress job, it's obviously wearing on you. You looked exhausted."

"I can't thank you enough, Mr. Lucas." Megan rose from her chair and beat a hasty retreat before he had time to change his mind.

Later, as she relayed the whole scene to Amy, what he had said dawned on her.

"He said he thought this whole thing had aged me. Well, he didn't say aged exactly, but that's what he meant. But that can't be true, I've been using that Dragon's Blood every morning and night. I think I've gone through more than a half a dozen jars."

Amy sighed. "I'm sorry to have to say it, but the long hours, the stress, the smoke in that awful bar, did have a negative effect on your skin. You look a little worn."

"Maybe a different kind of skin cream …?

THE INHERITANCE

Kathy carefully ran a dust cloth over the cream and gold oval surface of the teapot. The green dragon heads, which served as handles, seemed to be looking right at her. Kathy's mother had given the teapot to her while packing up to move out of the rickety old house that had been their home growing up.

"As the oldest daughter, you should have this now, Kathy," her mother said. "It's brought me luck all these years, and now it's your turn. I'm afraid something might happen to it if I take it with me to the community residence. It's been in our family for several generations, passed down from mother to daughter. I want you to have it and give it to little Stephanie some day, when she is grown with a family."

"Mom. I'm not sure I want the responsibility," Kathy said. "I'm sure it's very valuable, and you know the kids. They're pretty rambunctious." To herself, she wondered what good luck her mother meant. All she could remember was a drunken father who lashed out at the nearest person when he was angry. He had died early on in a car accident, and her mother had struggled to raise her and her two sisters on a limited income. The three of them had managed to get college educations with the help of scholarships and by taking part time jobs while in school. Now, in comfortable circumstances, they had been able to chip in on a nice apartment in an assisted-living home for their mother. She certainly deserved a comfortable place to live after all she had sacrificed for them.

"Just put it up high away from their reach. I'm sure it will be fine."

"Okay, if that's what you want." Kathy wrapped the set in tissue, slipped it into a grocery bag, gave her mother a hug, and headed home. She didn't know where she would display it, and she wasn't even sure she liked it. The dragons' faces were slightly menacing, but if they brought good luck, she could certainly use it.

"What's that, Mommy?" Stephanie asked when she saw Kathy putting the tea set on the buffet.

"It's an antique. We have to make sure we don't break it because it's supposed to bring us good luck," Kathy answered. "Some day it will be yours."

"Good luck? Like Daddy coming back home?"

"I don't think it's that good, honey, but we'll see." Kathy's husband, Mike, had left six months earlier to move in with a twenty-something blonde secretary named Angela. He had met her at work and been immediately infatuated.

"I love you, honey, just not in the same way," he'd said. "Don't worry though, I'll still provide for you and the kids."

That had sounded good at the time, but checks had been few and far between in the last couple months, and the kids complained about never seeing their father. Kathy sighed and ran her fingers through her hair. She didn't see how she was going to manage. Her job at a local gift shop didn't pay much, and she hadn't been able to find anything else.

Looking at the dragon teapot, she said, "If you were really good luck, you'd get rid of that Angela once and for all so that Mike will come back to us."

Two days later, her best friend, Sue called.

"Did you hear the news?"

"No, what?"

"Angela is dead."

"What! How?"

"Drowned in the pool attached to their apartment."

"Was it foul play?"

"I guess not. She couldn't swim. Looks like she tripped over the pool cleaning equipment and fell in, hit her head on the cement. No one else was around."

"Oh, my gosh! I didn't like her, but I wouldn't have wished her dead!"

The thought came to mind that she had asked the dragons to get rid of her permanently. Stupid. It was an accident pure and simple, and her talking to ceramic dragons had nothing to do with it. Still, now that Angela was gone, maybe she would get her husband back.

Kathy waited until after the funeral before calling him.

"Hi, Mike. It's Kathy. I was wondering how you were doing. We were all so sorry to hear about Angela's death."

"I'm still in shock. It doesn't seem real. I'm taking some time to get my head on straight, but I'll try to drop by to see the kids next week."

"So, you're going to stay in the apartment?"

'For awhile. I think I need some 'alone' time. Anyway, it was nice of you to call. I'll let you know when I'm coming over."

Kathy heard female voices in the background.

"I've got to go now. Talk to you soon." He clicked his cell off.

Alone my foot! Kathy thought as she hung up. She looked over at the dragon teapot and said, "Well, that didn't work. Got any other ideas?"

It seemed they did.

When the phone rang, she was washing dishes. She grabbed a dishtowel and hurriedly dried her hands.

"Hello."

"Um, Kathy, it's Mike."

"Oh, hi, Mike." Her heart gave a little jump at his voice. She hadn't given up hope that they might still get back together. "What's up?"

"I kind of need your help."

"In what way?"

"Well, I was wondering if I could stay at the house for a few weeks while I recuperate."

"Recuperate?"

"Yeah, I went skiing last week, you know."

"No, I didn't know. I didn't even know you skied." Kathy wondered what that had cost. At least a new pair of shoes for one of the kids, probably more than one pair of shoes.

"Apparently, I don't. I broke my leg and am having a hard time getting around."

"And you want to come here so I can take care of you?"

"Something like that."

"Would that mean you're coming back for good?"

"We can talk about it."

On the one hand, Kathy was furious. How dare he think that he could just come and go whenever it suited him or whenever he needed help? On the other hand, it would be great for the kids to have him around, and, maybe once he came back, he'd see what he had been missing. She gave in.

"All right. When did you want to come?"

"Could you pick me up today?"

"Pick you up? No, take a cab. I'll be here." Kathy slammed the phone down. Pick him up? What nerve.

An hour later, she heard a car in the driveway and car doors slam. She went to the front door and opened it. Mike came hobbling up the sidewalk on crutches.

"Could you get my bags? I can't carry them and manage these things, too."

What could she say? She went to the car and picked up two large suitcases, which the cab driver had set on the ground. By the time she had dragged them into the house, Mike was comfortably ensconced in the big lounge chair and had clicked on the television.

"I'm putting you in the guest room," she said.

"That's fine. Do you have any beer?"

"There's some in the fridge."

"Can you get it for me? I'm sorry, but walking is really difficult."

Was she expected to fetch and carry for him throughout his whole recovery time?

"How long will you be in that cast?"

"About five weeks."

"How many?" Kathy almost screeched. "What about work?"

"I can do it from here. All I need is my computer and a phone."

Never was there a longer five weeks. The man couldn't do anything for himself. Her job required her to be on her feet all the time. Now when she got home, he was waiting with a list of things he needed done, plus he expected her to cook full meals at breakfast and dinner and barely condescended to make his own sandwiches at lunch time. She began to wonder why she wanted him back.

At long last, the cast came off, and Mike announced that now that he was able to get along on his own, he would be moving into the apartment.

"I thought we were going to talk about your moving back here," Kathy said.

"I don't think it would work out." Mike glanced down at his bags as if in a hurry to get out of the house.

"Why is that?"

"There's just too much going on here all the time. The kids coming and going, your work schedule. I need some space."

"I can quit work." Kathy hated herself for even saying it.

"No, no. Don't do that on my account. Let's just leave things like they are and see what comes of it."

Kathy heard a horn toot outside.

"Oh, here's Brenda with my car," Mike said.

Brenda? Where did she come from, and what had he been doing while she had been at work?

Kathy didn't even bother to ask, just turned away from him. She heard the front door open and close and car doors after that. Tears formed in her eyes, and she brushed them away. She'd be darned if she would cry over him. He was gone forever out of her life. She knew that now. She'd been a fool to think he would come back. Her eye fell on one of the dragon faces.

"I guess that's that. Lesson learned. Still I wouldn't call it good luck."

No answer from the dragon, just a glassy stare.

Several months passed, and Mike was a little more regular in his support checks. She heard from friends that he was seen around town with several attractive women but no particular one all the time. So, no demanding girlfriend, more money for the kids. She extended her hours at the retail store, and when she got home each day, she was too tired to even think about preparing dinner. She poured herself a much-deserved drink and sank into an easy chair. More often than not, she ordered pizza or Chinese takeout to the delight of her kids.

One night during her weekly call to her mother, she asked about the "good luck" the dragon tea set was supposed to have brought her.

"I mean, Mom, you haven't been particularly lucky in life, you know. It was a struggle to raise us kids all by yourself on such a meager income. Where did the good luck come in?"

"Honey, do you remember your dad?"

"Yes, but they aren't fond memories."

"I was desperate to break free from him, the abuse, the drinking. I couldn't see my way to leaving with no skills and three kids, so I stayed, but I was miserable all the time. When my mother gave me the tea set, he made fun of it. What was I going to do with a tea set, he sneered, lifting his pinky finger in mockery. 'Aren't you the hoity toity one?' And so on. And then, he obligingly killed himself driving while drunk. Drove right into a tree. I couldn't have lived with myself if he had killed someone else."

"What do you mean, lived with yourself? It wasn't your fault."

"Well, that was the good luck, dear. I asked the dragons to let me go free. And they did."

"I'm sure it was just an accident."

"If that's what you want to think. How's Mike by the way?"

"He's fine, I guess. Decamped as they say."

"You're better off without him in your life. Is he sending money for the kids?"

"Off and on, when he doesn't have an expensive girlfriend."

143

"I'm sorry to hear that. Oh, it's time for dinner. I don't want to be late. Love you. Call me soon."

"Goodnight, Mom," Kathy said to the dial tone.

The next morning as she passed the tea set, she said in a stern voice, "Don't get any ideas, dragons. Things are fine the way they are."

This was a slight exaggeration because she was just barely making ends meet and knew that the property taxes were coming due soon. She called Mike to remind him.

"I know, honey. I just don't think I can come up with the money right now. The extra cost of the apartment and my living expenses, you know."

She knew all right. All that dating and partying that her friends kept telling her about.

"Then, what am I to do?"

"I think it's time we think about selling the house. You can probably find a rental somewhere cheap."

"Sell? Rental? What about the kid's school? Their friends?"

"Oh, one school is the same as another. They'll adapt. Got to go." And he clicked off.

Kathy slumped down in a chair and buried her face in her hands. What was she going to do? Then, not really believing anything would happen, she looked at the dragons.

"Do your best, guys. I'm up a creek here."

Several weeks later, she rushed into the house having had to work extra hours. She never turned down overtime anymore. She still had a half hour before the kids got home. Just enough time to fix after-school snacks and change clothes. She saw the message light blinking on the answering machine and pushed the button.

"Mrs. Mansfield. This is Officer Tucker of the Sacramento Police Department. Could you please call me back at this number? I have some urgent news for you."

Kathy picked up the phone and dialed.

"This is Kathy Mansfield. An Officer Tucker called me and asked that I call back."

"Oh, yes, Mrs. Mansfield. I'll put you right through."

The next voice on the phone was a man.

"James Tucker, here."

"Hi. This is Kathy Mansfield. You asked me to call?"

Immediately his voice dropped and became solemn.

"Oh, yes, Mrs. Mansfield. I'm so sorry to have to tell you this. Your husband was killed earlier today. I understand you're separated, but I thought you should be informed."

"Oh, my gosh! How did it happen?"

"He was hit by a drunk driver around 2 a.m. He was rushed to the hospital, but he never regained consciousness. I'm so sorry."

"Thank you for letting me know. I'll-I'll have to tell the kids."

"We've released the body to the Smith Funeral Home. You can make arrangements for the service through them. I understand you're still legally married."

"Yes. I'll do that. Thank you for calling."

The service was quiet and simple. Friends and co-workers came to pay their respects. And, to her relief, no weeping ex-girlfriends showed up.

Exhausted after all the stress of the previous days, she sank into an easy chair, too tired to think about what she would do without any money, such as it was, coming in from him. He had a small insurance policy at work, which had gone to pay for the funeral. What was she going to do now? Selling the house seemed her only option. Just then, her cell phone chimed, and she picked up.

"Yes?"

"Mrs. Mansfield?"

"Yes."

"My name is Jack Otis. I am, or I was, Mike's lawyer."

"Oh, yes, I think he mentioned you."

"Well, I'm calling to let you know that we will be paying off his insurance policy to you in the next week or so."

"I thought he only had the policy at work."

"Oh, no. This policy was opened when your first child was born. He's kept up the payments ever since. Actually it was an automatic deduction from his account. He probably didn't even notice it."

"Oh, that's wonderful. I'm sort of strapped for money right now. How much is it?"

"A half million dollars."

"A half million dollars? That's not possible."

"Possible or not, that's what it is. I'll post a check to you this week. So sorry for your loss."

Shaking her head, Kathy sat in stunned silence. She looked up and saw a ray of light hit the eye of one of the dragons. For a second, it appeared to be winking at her.

THE MAGIC DRAGON TOY SHOP

Marie only noticed the shop when she was directly in front of the door. The Magic Dragon Toy Shop was tucked in between a candy store and a souvenir shop on a side street in Old Sacramento. Intrigued by the small store, she stepped in and was immediately overwhelmed by the number of dragons on display. There were stuffed animals and licensed plastic figurines from several animated feature films. Books about Puff lined the shelves along with CDs of the music. There were other toys available, but the overwhelming impression was of dragons, large and small, plush and plastic, musical and printed.

"Wow," Marie said. "This is truly an amazing store."

A voice from behind a slightly hidden counter said, "Thank you. It is fun, isn't it?"

"Oh, I didn't see you there."

"I know. Coming from the light into the store sort of hinders your vision. Do you like dragons?" The speaker was a short, squat woman of indeterminate age sporting a bad haircut and a number of wrinkles.

"Actually, I don't have much of an opinion on them either way. But I do believe they're good luck."

"They've been good luck for us," the woman said. "We opened the shop a few years back. In spite of our size, we've been quite successful."

"I can see why. There must be something for everyone here."

"We try. What can I help you with?"

"I wasn't actually looking for anything specific," Marie said, "but now that I'm here, maybe something for my granddaughter, Finnean. She'll be six in a couple weeks."

"We have this wonderful book of dragon stories. They're the right degree of difficulty for that age." The woman held up a beautifully illustrated book.

"I don't think I've ever seen that book before," Marie said, awed.

"It's rather a rare copy. Only one I have in the shop. But it's not terribly expensive. I'll be glad to discount it for you, if you want it."

Marie picked up the book and turned the pages. Each one was more elaborate and colorful than the last. Although not a pop-up book, some of the images appeared to jump off the page towards her. Once she had it in her hands, for some reason she couldn't bear to give it back. Even with the discount, it was more than she usually spent. Still, she decided to splurge.

"I'll take it," she said.

"Good choice. I know your granddaughter will love it." The woman rang up the sale and slid the book into a bag. "Please come see us again."

"I certainly will now that I've discovered you. I bet my grandson would love one of those plush dragons. He's only four."

"I'm sure he would. The perfect age for his very own dragon."

Two weeks later, Marie arrived at Finnean's birthday party carrying the book, now wrapped in brightly colored paper and decorated with artfully-tied ribbon. On top was a specially selected birthday card prominently displaying the number six.

When the presents were unwrapped, everyone oohed and aahed over the beautiful book, and Marie knew she had done herself proud with this gift.

As she was leaving, Finnean ran over and hugged her.

"Grandma, thanks so much. I love my book."

"You're more than welcome, sweetheart. I hope you have many fascinating hours reading the stories. Let me know what you think."

As it turned out, it wasn't long before she found out what they all thought about the book.

"Mom!" Her daughter's voice screeched over the phone. "Where did you get that book?"

"Why? What's the matter? I bought it at a toy store."

"Finnean won't read anything else. She says every night the dragons come to life. They take her on trips to other lands. Show her magical people and places."

"Sounds like she has a very active imagination. That's a good thing, isn't it?"

"No, no, no. It's not a good thing. She's obsessed. She won't put the book down. Carries it everywhere, even to school. Says she's afraid the dragons will leave, and she doesn't want them to disappear. Her schoolwork is suffering. She's not eating well. I don't know what to do."

"Can't you just take the book, set it aside? Out of sight, out of mind, you know. She'll forget about it."

"If I even touch it, she throws a tantrum."

"Can't you get it when she's asleep?"

"No, she clutches it to her even then. If I try to slip it out of her arms, she wakes up and holds on to it with all her might, kicking and screaming."

"Maybe you should give it some time. She'll probably lose interest in it eventually."

"Eventually? I can't wait that long. You have to do something."

"What can I do?"

"I don't know, but you have to come and get that book back from her. I mean it."

"Take back a gift?"

"Tell her it was a loan or something. Tell her you have to give it back to the fairies or whoever now."

"Let me think about it."

"Okay. But think fast. I'm losing my mind here."

Marie didn't know what to do. This was a situation she had never faced before. Come to think of it, it was probably a situation most people never faced. Still, it was a problem of her making, and she had to deal with it. She drove to her daughter's house, took a seat in the kitchen and waited for the school bus to deposit Finnean at the curb.

A few minutes later, the door burst open and Finn ran in.

"Mom, Grandma's car is here. Oh, hi, Grandma, I love, love, love the book you gave me."

"Hi, Sweetie. So I hear."

"It's the most wonderful, magical book in the whole wide world."

"Yes. That's why I'm here."

"What do you mean?

"It turns out that they sold me the book by mistake. It really belongs to a very high and mighty wizard, and he is very angry about it being gone. He's demanding that we return it this very minute. If we don't, something awful will happen."

Finn clutched the book to her chest.

"He can't have it."

"I'm sorry, honey, but I have to give it back. I know you love it, but at least you got to keep it for a little while, and I'll get you some new books to take its place."

"I don't want any other books. I only want this one."

"I know. But I have to give it back. How would you feel if your most prized possession was taken away under your nose? Wouldn't you be sad and upset?"

"What's a prized possession?"

"Um, like your banky. Or your favorite doll."

"Oh. I see. But I need it. I can't give it up."

"Honey, so does he. And more than you do. You've only had it a couple weeks. It was his for all of his life. He is so sad and lonely without it. He needs his dragon friends. You have lots of friends from school and the neighborhood. Think of him with no one. Can you find it in your heart to do this for him?"

"No."

"Honey, I'll be in an awful lot of trouble if I don't give it back. Would you do it for me?"

"I guess." Finn looked devastated and still held tightly to the book.

"You are truly a wonderful girl. Give me the book and I'll make sure that it gets to him."

Finally Finn held out the book, and Marie took it carefully from her.

"Thank you. I'm sure he will let you know how grateful he is."

"He'd better. It's only the most precious-ist thing I have." Tears streamed down her face as she ran to her room.

With a sigh of relief, Marie hurried back to her car with the book before Finn could change her mind. Such a lot of fuss over a book. Really! Still she felt terrible about having to take it away from her granddaughter, making her cry. She had meant well.

Once at home, she made up a scroll with gold seals and impressive language and mailed it to Finn. It was purportedly from the Wizard, honoring her for a deed of exceeding generosity in returning his most cherished possession, etc. She hoped that would be the end of it.

She called her daughter a week later. "How's she doing?"

"She's back to normal. Whatever hold the book had over her seems to have disappeared. She's very proud of her honorary scroll."

"Thank goodness."

The book sat idle on the coffee table where Marie had set it when she came home. After a week, she noticed it sitting there and decided she should put it away in case Finn came to visit and saw it there. However, curiosity got the better of her. She opened the book and began to read. Although each page was decorated with gold leaf and finely drawn images, the stories were rather mundane. She couldn't see what all the fuss was about. Maybe you had to be six.

On the other hand, her nightly dreams now revolved around dragons and other-worldly landscapes until she began to dread falling asleep at night. The nightmares increased in intensity, and she knew she had to do something about them. There was only one solution. She should have thought of it sooner. Return the book. She wasn't sure they would take it back, but, if necessary, she would simply give it to them.

A week later, she walked down the side street in Old Sac where she had first found the toy shop. At the end of the block, she realized that she must have passed it. She walked back, but there was no toy shop on the whole street. She checked the other side of the street. Nothing.

Maybe she had mixed up the streets. She ended up walking up and down every street in the Old Town. She even made several more trips in the weeks that followed, searching for the store. She asked at the Visitor's Center, but they had never heard of it.

With no other recourse, she put the dragon book, along with several other books she was no longer reading, into a bag and donated them to her local library for their book sale. It sits there waiting for just the right child to come along.

ABOUT THE AUTHOR

Teresa Leigh Judd resides in the northern California foothills with her partner, Ken, and big black cat, Max. She is a graduate of the University of Washington and is employed as a manufacturers' rep for a number of product lines. Her job keeps her busy driving through the many small towns in the Gold Country as well as northern Nevada.

She is a member of Sisters in Crime and has had a number of short stories published. Her story, "Quick on the Draw" won second place in the 2009 Deadly Ink contest. Her most recent story "Among Strangers" can be found in the Sacramento Sisters in Crime anthology, *The Best of Capitol Crimes*.

She is the mother of three busy children and the proud grandmother of five.

Find her on her website www.TeresaLeighJudd.com or contact at teresajudd11@gmail.com

Made in the USA
Charleston, SC
13 March 2015